a little wanting song

Cath Crowley

Alfred A. Knopf

New York

THIS IS A BORZOI BOOK PUBLISHED BY ALFRED A. KNOPF

All rights reserved. Published in the United States by Alfred A. Knopf, an imprint of Random House Children's Books, a division of Random House, Inc., New York. Originally published in different form in Australia by Pan Macmillan Australia in 2005 under the title *Chasing Charlie Duskin*.

Knopf, Borzoi Books, and the colophon are registered trademarks of Random House, Inc.

Visit us on the Web! www.randomhouse.com/teens

Educators and librarians, for a variety of teaching tools, visit us at www.randomhouse.com/teachers

Library of Congress Cataloging-in-Publication Data
Crowley, Cath.
[Chasing Charlie Duskin]
A little wanting song / Cath Crowley. — 1st American ed.
    p. cm.
"Originally published in different form in Australia by Pan Macmillan Australia in 2005 under the title Chasing Charlie Duskin."
Summary: One Australian summer, two very different sixteen-year-old girls—Charlie, a talented but shy musician, and Rose, a confident student longing to escape her tiny town—are drawn into an unexpected friendship, as told in their alternating voices.
ISBN 978-0-375-86096-6 (trade) — ISBN 978-0-375-96096-3 (lib. bdg.)—
ISBN 978-0-375-89703-0 (e-book)
[1. Friendship—Fiction. 2. Love—Juvenile fiction. 3. Self-esteem—Fiction. 4. Loneliness—Fiction.
5. Bashfulness—Fiction. 6. Musicians—Fiction. 7. Australia—Fiction.] I. Title.
PZ7.C88682Ch 2010
[Fic]—dc22
2009020305

The text of this book is set in 13-point Galena.

Printed in the United States of America
June 2010
10 9 8 7 6 5 4 3 2 1
First American Edition

To Nancy and Joe Davis, and to Jessie and Tom Crowley—

My beautiful grandparents

Charlie

Dad and I leave town in the early dark. It's the second Sunday of the holidays, and we pack up the old blue car with enough clothes for summer and hit the road. It's so early he's wiping hills of sand piled in the corners of his eyes. I wipe a few tears from mine. Tears don't pile, though. They grip and cling and slide in salty trails that I taste till the edge of the city. It's our first Christmas in the country since Gran died.

At six o'clock the sun rises and lights the car from the outside. Blinds us almost. Dad squints through his glasses at the road, but me? I close my eyes. I like things better when I listen. Everything in the world's got a voice; most people don't hear hard enough is all. Sunrise sounds like slow chords dripping from my guitar this morning. Sad chords, in B-flat.

"Open your eyes, Charlie love," Mum whispers. "You'll miss out on the day." Not a lot to miss out on, really. My days have been sort of shaky lately. Like a voice running out of breath. Like a hand playing the blues. Like a girl losing her bikini top in the pool at Jeremy Magden's final party for Year 10 last week, if we're getting specific. Mum says look on the bright side. Okay. I guess I was only half naked.

The thing that really kills is that the party started so well. I was talking and making jokes and the words were rolling easily, and I thought: I've done it. I've found that thing, whatever that thing is, that most people have but I don't.

"Check out Alex checking you out," Dahlia said, and we laughed. I felt good because it sounded like she wasn't mad anymore. And a guy was finally looking at me, not straight through to the other side. There was this beat under my skin, a little disco weaving through me. That's how it is when I'm alone and playing the guitar, but that's never how it is in a crowd.

Only, that day it was. I had the first line of a new song in my head. A song about a guy and a party and a smile. The words were in my mouth and the tune was in my blood, and it felt so loud I thought: If Alex kisses me, he'll hear it singing through my skin.

And I wanted him to hear. Because he grinned electricity through my bones, when most days I play solo and acoustic. Because Dahlia's new friends might like me if I had something other than music to talk about during Louise Spatula's post-party analysis.

"You look good. The sunglasses are working. You can do this," Dahlia told me. And I really thought I could. I was confident. I was ready.

"Just remember," Louise said, "a blow-up doll could get Alex."

I was stuffed. "Thanks. I won't keep that in mind." But I did keep it in mind. If things went badly, Louise would make sure everyone knew it and I'd be a step below plastic for the rest of my high school life. Dahlia took Louise inside so I wouldn't have an audience, but she did it too late. My disco disappeared. I walked across to Alex, humming a song I called "Fuck" because that was the only word in it.

The chorus was moving through my head and I was so busy humming I didn't see the football game. I walked straight through the middle. David Amar threw the ball; Joseph Ryan sprinted to get it and collected me on the way. I ran in front of him for a couple of seconds, and then I ducked and rolled into the pool. Unexpected, sure. But not entirely uncool.

It was kind of funny. Till I realized the force of the fall had loosened my bikini top and it was impossible to find in the middle of all the water-bombing that was going on around me.

Swimming along the bottom, I forced my eyes open and searched through legs. I could have done something creative with a couple of chip packets and a leaf at that point, but I had nothing. Absolutely nothing. Except a little voice inside me screaming out for one, just one, normal encounter with a guy. Or at least abnormal with clothes.

I figured my best chance was to move slow and hope no

one noticed. Usually that's the way it goes for me at parties so it wasn't like I was asking for a miracle. I raised myself out of the water and walked to where I'd left my towel. Louise was outside by then but I was elevator music behind her and she didn't notice a thing. I was feeling kind of lucky.

Till I saw a packet of tissues sitting on the chair where my towel had been. *A packet of freaking tissues.* I'm not entirely lacking in optimism, though. I pulled out a couple. My hair dripped and a second later they disappeared in my hands. Turns out "Fuck" is a song for all occasions.

"Oh my God, Charlie, your boobs are hanging out!"

"No shit, Louise," I said as every boy in Jeremy's backyard fired up his tracking equipment and locked his eyes onto my chest. "Boobs" is one of those words, like "fire" or "gun" or "free money." You just have to look.

And Alex looked.

And Jason Taylor let out this squealing laugh and Louise joined in and then so did everyone else. "You should have shown me the bikini in the fitting rooms at the shop," Louise said as she stretched out on her towel. "I would have told you not to buy it."

And that was it. I was sucked into the Louise Spatula time machine and spat out into Year 3 where I'm handing over coins to kids because she told them I should pay to be their friend. I remembered Dahlia saying to me in Year 5, "From now on, *they* pay *you*."

Her eyes said the same thing at Jeremy's party as she handed me a towel. I took my clothes to the bathroom. I stared in the mirror for a while. I did that thing where you turn and spin back and try to catch yourself by surprise. See you how the world does. How a guy called Alex might. Not spectacular, sure. But not entirely unspectacular.

I got dressed and walked back to the pool thinking, Stuff you all. You've seen my skin, big deal. Big fucking deal. Unless you were born wearing designer jeans and T-shirts, someone's seen yours, too. I planned on saying exactly that, only Louise got in first. "Welcome back, four-eyes."

It was breathtaking, and in the worst kind of way: it took my breath. Jason pig-laughed again and Dahlia shifted her towel toward Louise. "Your hair's dripping on me, Charlie," she said. I told her I was leaving and she told me goodbye. Not see you tomorrow or see you later. Goodbye. A flat, hard endnote.

Dahlia came to my school a few weeks into Year 5 and we clicked. I hadn't clicked with anyone before her. I don't know why. Maybe it was because there was never an even number of kids in the class and I was too shy to push into a pair.

Being on my own before Year 4 wasn't so bad. On the bright side I never had to share my lunch, which was always first-class since my dad's a chef and he made it every day. But I came back from the summer holidays pretty desperate for a friend.

Dahlia heard me one lunchtime, playing my guitar. I was sitting on the steps near the classroom, doing this cover of a Johnny Cash song Mum had taught me. "How come you're sitting on your own?" she'd asked.

I said, "Just because." And switched to a song I knew she knew and she hung around. Dahlia couldn't play an instrument but she could really belt out a tune.

And she could eat my dad's chocolate cake faster than anyone I ever saw. "Watch this," she said that first day. "I can eat and sing at the same time." She shoved a fist-sized piece of cake into her mouth and sang what I think was Madonna. Kids stared, we were laughing so hard. She didn't care what they thought of me. "Charlie's funny," she said. "And you're all boring."

We'd have these sleepovers at my place where we'd turn up the radio and sing ourselves raw. We wouldn't stop till Dad came in about three. Dahlia would freeze. Superwoman pajamas on, hairbrush microphone in hand, she'd ask, "Any requests, Mr. Duskin?" She took the quiet in our house and smashed it.

Things were great till Louise came onto the scene. The teacher put her next to Dahlia in a class seating plan in Year 9 and things took off from there. Dahlia says she's nicer than people think, but surveys taken suggest the opposite. Being dead is better than being the enemy of Louise—just ask Andrew Moshdon.

One afternoon on the bus last year Louise said, "Can you move, please, Andrew? I want to sit next to Dahlia."

"Don't see your name on the seat." He turned his face to the window. Kids all around heard. Greg Forego whistled low. Andrew was a dead man.

Next week at the school sports carnival he pissed in the

pool, so the story went. Only he wasn't anywhere near the water. He sat with me all day at the timer's desk, laughing at my jokes and lending me his hat. The boys started calling him pisshead and the girls called him pig. Most guys would have gotten away with it, but Andrew was different. Andrew read in the library at lunchtime. He hated football. He was depending on Charlie Duskin to help him.

The day after the rumors started he grabbed me in the hall. "I've been looking for you everywhere. I need you to tell people the truth about sports day." He was talking like I could save him.

I stared at his face and I knew what he felt and I said, "I wasn't with you every minute of the day, Andrew." He only looked confused for a second.

Later in Year 9 he became the kid who farted in class. In Year 10 he was the guy who spat when he talked. I couldn't have stopped it, even if I'd told, and telling meant pissing off Louise and losing Dahlia.

I lost her anyway.

I walked home the long way after Jeremy's pool party. I hoped that if I took my time, there'd be a message waiting for me when I got in the door. A year ago Dahlia would have called and said something like "In the name of science, I have to know. What's it like to be naked in front of a guy?"

I would have said something back like "I don't know, but in the name of romance I'm hoping it feels better than being naked in front of fifty guys."

There was no message. For years I've been Dahlia's second half. I guess things change, though, so slowly you don't notice the chord's different. You're playing B7 with added D and then D drifts away and all you're left with is B minor. That's a pretty sad key.

So I pulled out my guitar case, cold and dimpled like the skin of an orange. I practice for hours most days, more when I'm sad. I click the clasps and peel back the lid and underneath it's sweet. I play till the sound fills me, rich and gold and warm like the wood. It's my voice: smooth and unscratched. I sing when no one else is there. I sing, beautiful and in tune. Pity I didn't have my guitar with me at the pool; I could have used it for cover.

I sat there after the party, singing some tunes and thinking about how I'd treated Andrew Moshdon last year. I looked up his number in the phone book and stared at it for ages, wondering about the best thing to say to a guy after you left him for dead and didn't bother to look back till over a year later. Nothing sounded right so I rang and played it by ear.

"Hey, Andrew. It's Charlie," I said, and all I got back was breathing. "Charlie Duskin."

"I know who you are."

"So. So you weren't at the pool party today."

"That's funny, Charlie. I can hardly talk I'm laughing so hard."

"I didn't mean . . . I know you didn't do that last year." But there's no good way to tell someone you believe they didn't piss in the pool.

"I have to go."

"You want funny," I said before he could hang up, "try losing your bikini top in front of almost every guy in Year Ten."

There was one beat of quiet and then he said, "I don't wear bikinis."

"Yeah, well, lucky you."

And then I told him everything, about Alex and the skin disco, about the footy game and the tissues and Louise. I even sang him my song called "Fuck." Andrew's got a very cool laugh. I'd forgotten that.

We made up a new song together. One about Louise. Turns out more words than you think rhyme with Spatula. "Sometimes singing makes you feel pretty good," I said before I hung up.

"You should sing it to her."

"Yeah," I told him, in a way that could mean a few things.

Jeremy's party was a week ago and Dahlia hasn't called once since then. I check my phone as we hit the freeway. Still nothing. Dad merges at the wrong speed and for a second I think it's all over but then the cars around give us a lane to ourselves and Dad can drive any way he wants without horns blaring. The sign says we've got a while to go till we get there. Three hundred kilometers. The paper says it's burning hot all over Australia today. The heat and Dad's driving and the lack of messages on my phone make me feel like we've got a thousand kilometers ahead of us. At least.

Rose

This place is as quiet as a ghost town on Sunday mornings. Ever since Year 7 I've come to the edge of the freeway on my own to watch the cars passing. The only noises are the birds and the wind and the people coming and going. Everyone drives through on the way from one place to another. No one ever stays.

I don't blame them. Of all the places in the world I could have been born, I got the drink and toilet stop capital of the world. Like my boyfriend, Luke, says, you got to be pissed about that. I am pissed about it. Some days I'm so pissed I throw rocks at the cars driving out because they get to leave and I don't.

"You'll go if you want to, Rose," Mrs. Wesson, my Year 10

science teacher, said this year. It takes a lot of wanting to get out of a place like this, though. It takes wanting so bad it's all you care about, all you dream about, all you breathe. Some days I think it takes more wanting than I've got.

The stupid thing is I should have been born somewhere else. Mum and Dad did it in the backseat of his car the night before she left on this big overseas trip she'd been planning for ages. I was on a plane to London before I was a heartbeat. I was out of here. Then she brought me back.

She waited till the beginning of this year to tell me that important piece of information. We were coming home from the driving-test place after I'd got my learner's permit and I was going on and on about how jealous Luke and Dave would be when she blurted out, "I got pregnant in the back of a car, you know." I nearly steered us into the path of an oncoming truck.

"Shut up, Mum." Who wants to think about their parents having sex?

"I just don't want you to do anything stupid, Rosie," she said, and I turned on the windscreen wipers even though it hadn't rained for weeks.

"I'm not planning on it." I gripped the wheel tight. The only driving I planned on doing was the sort that got me to the city. The car filled up with quiet and I took the shortcut home.

I went to my room as soon as we got back. I didn't want to talk about what Mum had told me, but she crept in later. She laid her head on the pillow beside me and her breath stole the cool of the night. I kept my eyes closed and pretended to sleep.

"You weren't a mistake," she told me before she shut my door. But I was. Things might have been different for her if she'd kept going, if she hadn't come back to a place still as air, a place where nothing happens. Things might have been different for me.

When I was young, Mum and Dad made things exciting. They took chances. They watched sunrises. We'd walk through the dark, Mum's fingers wrapped tight around mine, Dad's coat brushing my knees. We were the only three people awake in a world half asleep and the air felt heavy with maybe. I knew any minute the sun would explode and color would spread across the sky. When I was about six, we stopped going. "We're tired, love. How 'bout we have a lie-in?"

I once heard Mum talking to her friends, saying, "Rose is exactly the same as me when I was young." You're wrong, I wanted to scream at her. I won't turn out like you. I won't think I've hit the big time because I've worked my way up from caravan park cleaner to caravan park manager. I won't stop reading books and start reading supermarket catalogs.

In Year 7 I started talking about the things I'd read to Miss Cantrell, my science teacher. She was the one who gave me the book on the cormorants in Brazil, long black lines swooping along the rivers, birds born to fly. Far out on the edges of the Pacific, the book said, there was another type of cormorant. These birds were almost exactly like the ones that lived in Brazil, except that they'd forgotten how to use their wings. "Why did they forget?" I asked her in class.

"Evolution, Rose," she answered. "Their bodies change over time. They don't need to fly to get food, or to move to warmer climates, so they don't."

Miss Cantrell went back to the city at the end of Year 7. I guess she couldn't stand this place, either. "It's not that, Rose," she said, packing up her things. "I've loved it here. It's time to move on, that's all. Who knows—maybe I'll come back someday." I picked up the book on the cormorants and traced the black lines of their wings. "You keep that," she said, and clipped her bag shut.

I started watching sunrises on my own after she left. I rode to the freeway and looked for her old yellow Holden every Sunday. I hoped every time I saw a yellow car coming toward me and I stopped hoping every time it flew past. I kept going long after I knew she wasn't coming back, like I've watched the colors explode in the sky long after I knew they weren't real. Just reflections of light.

I'd stopped hoping that things would change for me—until this year. Mrs. Wesson said I should try out for a scholarship in the city. "It's at a great school for science, Rose. You'd love it," she told me in June. If I won the scholarship, I could start in Year 11, next year.

"I don't think Mum and Dad would let me," I said. I knew they wouldn't. I'd asked them last year if I could apply for an exchange to Italy. "You're a bit young, Rosie," Mum said. She didn't even stop what she was doing to look at the flyer. She kept right on slicing carrots into sticks that looked the same.

"Why don't you check?" Mrs. Wesson asked. "The exam is in a month. You'd have to sit for it at the school. I could drive

13

you if they sign a permission form." She pulled one out of her drawer and passed it to me along with the application to sit the exam. "You're ready, Rose. You're one of my brightest students."

Mrs. Wesson called me into her office a week after she'd given me the form. The walls were lined with fake wood. The windows were nailed shut to stop kids from stealing stuff. Her car keys sat in a glass dish on the desk. How could she understand what it was like? She could get up and drive out of here tomorrow if she wanted. I handed her my application with forged signatures. "You don't need to drive me."

On the day of the exam, Dave and Luke thought I was home sick. Mum and Dad thought I was at school. I took a bus and then a train, and as soon as I saw that place, saw the girls in their uniforms and the huge library and the computer rooms, I knew I belonged there. The desks weren't graffitied with "Fuck you." The only drawings of anatomy were hanging on the wall. I sat at the station that afternoon feeding small birds, dreaming that I lived in the city. I let three trains leave before I took one home.

I found out for sure that I was accepted last month. Mrs. Wesson waved the results and her laughter ribboned out. "Your parents will be so proud." It must have been my face that made her voice fade to a thread. "Rose, how did you get there?" she asked. Her hand was already on the phone. "Don't look away. Did you forge their signatures?"

"You don't know them," I said, staring out the window at the tired trees. She stared with me. "I grew up in this town, too," she said. "Let me talk to them. The interview's in the fifth week of the holidays. I'll be gone for the start of summer, but I can help you tell them before I leave."

"If you do that, then it's over. I have to explain."

I went to the caravan park after school. "What would you think of me moving to the city next year if I could get a scholarship?"

"I'd think you're too young," Mum said. "Where would you live?"

"Maybe I could do some sort of exchange thing or share a flat with someone. I'll be Year Eleven."

"You've been in more trouble this year than ever, Rosie."

"Because of Luke."

"Plenty of Lukes in the city. Plenty worse than him."

I stared at the stack of cleaning products piled in the corner of her office while her voice ran on forever around me. "You'll be gone soon enough. Two years. Have a little patience."

I swung my bag and hit that stack and I didn't stop to pick it up. Fuck you, I thought as she called after me. I raced across paddocks to the freeway. I yelled and threw rocks and dreamed of ways I could take that scholarship without her help. I didn't stop throwing till I heard my name. "Rose."

"Constable Ryan."

He took me back to the caravan park and gave Mum a warning.

"I should let you go to the city, that's exactly what I should do," she said after he'd gone, slamming her stack of cleaning products back into place. "It won't be a warning next time. I'll be visiting you in prison. Looking for f—" Her hands strangled the air. "For lawyers."

"Fucking lawyers, Mum. That's what you mean. And as if you'd help me escape."

"With that mouth they wouldn't let you into a private school."

I almost told her then. I almost yelled, They did let me in, because they like my mouth. But that would have ruined everything. So I shut my smart mouth and we didn't talk till we got home. "You're always pushing," Mum said, and walked inside.

I thought if I knew someone in the city, and if I stayed out of trouble, maybe, maybe Mum might change her mind. It was a long shot, but before school finished I asked at the office if they had a number where I could reach Miss Cantrell.

They hadn't heard from her since she left, either. She hadn't paid a visit since she taught me science in Year 7. If she hasn't come back to town by now, she never will. It doesn't take a scholarship winner to work that one out. No one's coming to save me from this place. That's why I have to save myself, whatever it takes.

Charlie

"I wonder how Davie Robbie's doing," Mum says, and it's her way of telling me things aren't all bad. She makes a good point. I might be headed to a place where my gran won't be standing at the door. I might be facing a summer full of nothing to do and no friends to do it with. But at least the scenery in that country town is not entirely bad. If Dave Robbie's a song, he's written in major chords.

He's got this way of smiling that makes me want to throw him down and kiss him. And yeah, I know that any guy I have to throw down to kiss probably isn't Mr. Right. Still. I can dream.

Mum's always hinting I should ask him out, but when a girl finds talking as hard as I do and singing in public even harder, that leaves mime and interpretative dance. Don't get me wrong. I'd be great at both those things, but I don't think Dave's all that into the arts.

He does talk to me more than the other kids in town, though. His best friends, Rose and Luke, act like I'm invisible half the time and the other half they act like I'm that mysterious thing that messes with their TV reception. Rose Butler could be Louise Spatula's slightly less evil twin. Every time we arrive in town she's sitting on the hill like a bad omen. "Maybe she's lonely," Mum says. Maybe. She isn't lonely for me.

She'd avoid me completely, only Grandpa lives at the back of the shop and she lives next to it. Plus, our milk bar is one of only two places to eat at lunchtime. We sell all the usual stuff, like groceries and papers, but Grandpa also makes the best takeaway food in town. There's a section out the front where he has plastic chairs and tables. He never bothers to take the furniture inside, so sometimes Rose and Luke and Dave haunt the front of the shop till they're shadows.

Last summer Dave came in and ordered chips for the three of them while Luke and Rose waited outside. He smiled and that was more than enough reason to double their serves and not charge extra. I even gave them some little packets of tomato sauce for free.

I put the food on the table and Rose ignored me completely and I thought, Shit, country kids are even more hard-core than the ones in the city. Who doesn't crack a smile when you give them free chips?

"You want something?" Rose asked.

Sure, I thought. A little gratitude. World peace. A new acoustic guitar. A bass guitar and hands that play like Flea from the Red Hot Chili Peppers. Natalie Merchant and Gabriel Gordon's unreleased single, "Break Your Heart," which is proving pretty hard to find. We don't always get what we want.

I couldn't say that, though. Not with Luke and Rose and Dave and some other kids from the town all staring at me. If I said that and they said something else and I didn't have a comeback, it could get out of control. I gave them a look with a little attitude, though. Sort of like Shirley Manson, the singer from Garbage, that time she lost it onstage.

"It freaks me out how she stares and doesn't say anything," Rose said as I walked away.

"I bet it freaks her out how you're a bitch sometimes, too," Dave said.

I went inside and found a song on my iPod with a hard bass line and a whole lot of drums and I let the music rip a hole in the world, one that I could walk through and be somewhere else for a while.

I looked up from that other place and saw Dave staring through the glass. I thought: That guy is a little gratitude, world peace, a new acoustic guitar, a bass guitar and hands that play like Flea, and the single "Break Your Heart" all at once. He smiled and waved. I'm sick of staring at what I want, I thought. I'd do anything to hold it in my hands.

Rose

I'm not alone at the freeway for long this morning. "Rose," Luke yells from the edge of the field. "Today, Rose." He and Dave get so excited in the first week of summer holidays. It rolls out in front of them like a long sleep. It feels like a coma to me.

Luke gives me a whole lot of shit over how much I like school. He gives me a whole lot of shit over most things these days, but I don't care. I like knowing why dark clouds crack at the end of a day hot as fever. I like knowing why rain falls. I like Mrs. Wesson.

"How come we have to read all this crap?" Luke always asks ten minutes into every science lesson.

"Because she says," I tell him. "So shut up, I'm trying to concentrate." He waits for a bit, then steals my pen and flicks my hair till usually I do something like walk over to the window, wind it open, and throw his books into the yard.

"I expect more from you, Rose," Mrs. Wesson says when I do that, and I feel bad because I want to give her more. So I go back to my seat and kick Luke in the ankle and he yells so loud that more often than not I get a detention.

"You're lucky I didn't kick you higher," I whisper. I don't talk to him for the rest of the class and he feels so bad he goes up to Mrs. Wesson at the end and says, "It was me as well as Rose." Then Dave tells her it was him, too, because if we're stuck at school he might as well be. She sighs. "It looks like I've got the three of you again."

Almost every time we're kept in Luke tries to escape early. "Come on. She's not looking, let's go," he writes on a note and slips it across the table.

"Luke Holly. That had better be a note about science," Mrs. Wesson says, still staring at her work. There are only three of us in the room, genius. You don't think she'd notice us gone?

Even in primary school Luke had a reputation for being the kind of kid teachers hate. He got into fights all the time. Once he gave Daniel Mooper a black eye because Daniel had asked me to be his partner in tennis. Mr. Booth was yelling that he was suspending Luke and Luke was yelling back, "What? He started it. As if he doesn't know I'm her partner and Dave's backup."

Once kids get reputations like Luke's, teachers blame them for everything. He's had more detentions than Dave and me put together and we've had a fair few. The thing is in Year 9 teachers started looking for reasons to get Luke kicked out of school. A lot of students in our town leave at the end of Year 10. Some find apprenticeships or start working with their parents.

Mrs. Wesson's been trying to convince Luke to leave for his own good. "I'm not fucking dumb," he told her when she said he might try a trade instead of doing Year 12. She looked at him and said, "My husband's a plumber. He's not fucking dumb." It's the only time I've seen Luke with nothing to say. Mrs. Wesson's on his side. She's about the only teacher who is.

Luke's running out of chances. He keeps doing stupid stuff, like nicking off at the aquarium excursion earlier this year. If someone other than Mrs. Wesson had noticed, he would have been sent to the principal for sure.

"Come on, Rosie," he said as soon as we got inside, "there are at least fifty kids here. We could sneak off easy and look round the city for a bit."

"Are you crazy? The teachers would kill us."

"As if. They'd maybe hurt us a little. C'mon."

"No." I'd been looking forward to that day for ages. I wanted to see all of the things we'd been reading about in class. That was fun to me but Luke didn't get it.

"Do whatever you like, Luke."

"I will," he said.

"Dickhead," I shot back. Things are bad with your boyfriend when every conversation ends with "Do whatever you like. I will. Dickhead."

I watched him drift to the back of our group and edge away from Mrs. Wesson. I kept hoping he wouldn't really do it, because I knew that if he walked out that door, Dave and I would go with him.

"If Luke jumped off a cliff, you'd jump after him," Mum always says when he gets me into trouble. She's right, but every time I see Luke doing something stupid, the only thing I want to do is save him. He smiles and I do anything he asks.

I felt sick as I watched him that day. He was an expert at cutting. First he got real quiet, then he slouched his shoulders a bit and stuck his hands into his pockets. He dropped his head till he looked like one of the class nerds. No one even noticed him moving slowly away from our group to stand behind the kids at the baby shark and stingray pool.

"Does anyone know how the North Pacific sea star reproduces?" our guide asked.

"They rip themselves in half," I said. "Divide into two."

He smiled at me. "And why would they do that?"

"Maybe they couldn't find another star to mate with," I said. In the background Luke wiggled his fingers in the water at the tiny sharks. Or maybe the stars they had to choose from were idiots.

"Right. It's Rose, isn't it?" he asked, and I nodded. "It's pretty stressful, though, tearing yourself in two. It's better to find another star to reproduce with if they can."

"You know, this would be a perfect place for you to do work experience," Mrs. Wesson whispered, and I whispered back that I'd been thinking exactly the same thing.

23

"So why else is it better to mate with another star rather than just divide?" The guide kept firing questions as Luke moved farther away. We'd read in class last week that if they divide they end up with kids who are exact copies of them. I remembered thinking maybe that would make some of the parent stars happy. Sometimes it feels like Mum wants me to be exactly like her, stay at home and get married like she did.

"Dave," I said, and elbowed him in the ribs. "Look." He followed the direction of my eyes and saw Luke edging out the door.

"Is he crazy?"

"Yes," I said. "I think he is."

"What are we going to do?" Dave asked.

"Get expelled?"

"What's another problem with tearing yourself in two?" the guide asked as Dave and I moved slowly toward the entrance. I couldn't believe no one knew the answer. Tearing anything in half hurts, you idiots, doesn't it?

Luke was waiting for us outside. He knew all along I'd follow him. I grabbed his shirt. "They'll know you're gone. You think they're stupid?"

"Relax, Rose."

"We need to go back."

"I'm not ready yet. There's a McDonald's near the station." Luke was dangerous when he got like this. I looked at my watch; they'd do a head count soon.

"Luke, c'mon."

"Why don't you all come on," Mrs. Wesson said. That woman had a knack for busting the three of us. "Luke, you come with me. Rose, you and Dave don't leave Mr. Felder's side for the rest of the day."

Everyone else got free time to explore the aquarium in the afternoon. I had to shadow a teacher. "Tell me about the sharks, Rosie," Dave said, trying to cheer me up.

"Well, you can't tell how dangerous they are from their size. That's all wrong. The big ones don't always feed on meat."

"How do you tell a dangerous one?" he asked.

"Their teeth."

"So what, you ask them to smile?"

"If you're stupid enough to come in close and see them smile," I said, thinking of Luke, "then you deserve everything you get."

Mum heard about what happened at the aquarium, because everyone hears everything in this town. "If Luke jumped off a cliff, I swear you'd jump with him," she said again. I watched her slam cupboards shut. And I knew there wasn't any point in asking her about work experience in the city.

Charlie

"Will you miss Gran?" I ask Dad at the edge of town.

He doesn't shift his gaze from the road ahead. "My mum was old, and it was time." If he wasn't driving, he'd reach for his wallet. Usually when he doesn't know what to say, he gives me money to buy CDs. I've got a music collection that takes up an entire wall of my room. Bach to Veruca Salt and everything good in between.

I work after school at Old Gus's Secondhand Record and CD Store, so I get first pick when the good stuff comes in. Gus teaches me the guitar. When he's busy, sometimes his wife, Beth, gives me singing lessons. She's the one who told me what software and keyboard I needed to record my own music. It took a whole lot of saving and saying things to Dad like "Let's talk about the birds and the bees," but I got the money.

I packed everything in the trunk this morning. Computer, keyboard, iPod, dock, CDs that I haven't had time to load, this nifty little record player I found at a flea market, my favorite records. "Do you have everything, Charlotte?" Dad asked before he started the car. I've been getting the urge lately to say things that mean something to see if Dad gets it, so I said, "All I've got is in the trunk." He nodded and started the car and I thought about me and him. Words floated in my head like they do when I'm getting an idea for a song. Words like smoke and rain.

"See if you can find anything on the radio," Dad says after I ask about Gran.

I search around for a station. "Nothing but empty air." I replay the CD mix I made for the trip.

I'll miss Gran enough for both of us. She always took a little time off from the milk bar when I visited. I'd play songs for her while she hung out washing or worked in the garden. I sang softly while the smell of lavender drifted across the day. Gran's favorite was this cover I did of a Pink Daze track, "Smashed-Up World." Watching her get on down to the explicit version, I used to say that old people don't always lose their groove. But then sometime the year before last she lost it and seven months ago she died.

Most years I stay in the country till about halfway through January. Dad heads back to the city after Boxing Day. "I have to work," he says, starting the car before he's kissed me goodbye. I watch him drive away and I can almost taste the chocolate cake someone else'll be eating.

This Christmas he's taken time off from the restaurant to

help Grandpa over the busy season, so we're here together till the twentieth of January. Six extra days might not seem like a lot but it's a long time in this place without friends or Gran. It's a long time if Dahlia keeps up the silent treatment she started last week and doesn't call or text me this summer.

"Who's this?" Dad asks when a catchy tune comes on my CD. We pass the skeleton tree that never has leaves, no matter what the time of year. Bare gray branches wave us on. "No one you know, Dad," I say.

It's me.

Rose

Luke keeps skimming my name across the feathered grass. I hate being interrupted at the freeway. It's my time to be alone, my time to think. Lately, I've got a whole lot of things to think about, like how I'm getting out of here at the end of summer. I know I won't be asking Luke or Dave to help me think of a plan. That'd be a quick way to stuff up everything.

"Stop yelling, Luke. I heard you the first time."

He's still shouting when I see the dusty blue Ford coming toward me. Another boring summer full of people like boring Charlie Duskin. I watch her car pull into the gas station on the edge of town. She arrives every year carrying this guitar she never plays, hanging around with her iPod on and looking like the world's about to end. I'd give anything to leave this town after the holidays. I'd even trade places with her if it meant I could go to that school in the city.

"Today, Rose," Luke shouts, turning his bike back in the direction he's come from. "Meet us at the bus stop out front of the milk bar."

I don't move straightaway. I close my eyes and imagine what it would feel like to be in that car instead of here. To know that at the end of the holidays my dad and I would escape. "I'm leaving at the end of summer." I say it aloud to make it real. I want there to be witnesses, even if it's only the cars and the road and the sun. When I get scared about what I have to do, I'll think about the cormorants. I'll remember what happens when you're born in a place where you don't need to fly. I stay until Luke's voice echoes again. And then I open my eyes and pick up my bike and head back the way I came. Just like every other day.

Charlie

Rose is still on the hill when Dad pulls into the gas station. Luke and Dave rip past me, Dave riding without hands so he can wave. She rides past later, eyes ahead, both hands on the bars.

I used to watch them when I came for the summer. They'd play cricket with the kids from the street in Rose's backyard and I'd sit in Gran's old plum tree because I could see it all from there.

"Why don't you go on over?" Gran asked once when she found me. Because Rose had red silk for hair. Because she laughed like a trumpet, mellow and sweet as mango. She had two boys for best friends and always decided what the three of them would do. She'd say, "Let's go to the river," and Luke and Dave followed. I sat high in the branches and dreamed of someone following me like that. I wanted someone to look at me the way Luke looked at her.

When I was in Year 7, I heard them talking out the front of the shop. "Piss off, Luke," Rose said, and he brushed his hair back from his face and smiled. He followed her like a long dress dragging in the dirt.

When I told someone to piss off, they did. I know because in Year 8 I told Ayden Smith and he never spoke to me again. "Why'd you say that?" Dahlia asked. "You sort of liked him, didn't you?"

"It worked for Rose Butler," I said, and Dahlia looked at me the same way she always did back then. As if I was crazy but she didn't mind. "Well, Rose Butler's wrong. There are rules with boys, and one of them is, if you want them to stick around, don't tell them to get lost."

Sure, it made sense. But it wasn't what I wanted to hear. I wanted her to tell me there was some way to be like Rose, some way to be a girl who doesn't follow the rules. Gran invited her and Luke and Dave over one summer at the end of Year 8. She made sandwiches and cake and we sat in the living room. Rose didn't eat. She didn't talk. She kicked the legs of the chair she was sitting on and glared out the window.

Dave was the only one who spoke to me. "Thanks for the food." He walked to the gate before he turned back. "Rose is only mad because she hates doing what her mum tells her!" he yelled, and ran after them down the street.

I liked how Dave smiled at me before he ran and how his hair hung around his face, half falling in his eyes. I liked that he let Rose bowl him out in summer cricket and laughed when the guys gave him a hard time for it. He hangs behind Luke and Rose like the backbeat to a song. They need him there, though; he fits, and he knows it.

I wouldn't mind sitting next to Dave on a day when the sky's a lazy blue. I wouldn't mind singing him a song where the backbeat is the front beat. A song about a girl who's been holding it all in for years and finally finds a way to let it all out.

"Ready?" Dad asks, getting back in the car.

"Oh yeah. I'm ready."

Mum's the one who understands what I really mean when I say things like that. I cried with her when I got the news about Gran. She was the one who told me to sing "Smashed-Up World" and sing it loud. I did. I punched it at the air before Dad got home. Punched it at the world. Cracked it out till there was no sound left, just an ache in my throat. Mum wouldn't tell. She's good at keeping secrets. She should be.

She's been dead for seven years.

I was nine years old when it happened. I walked out of school and Dad was sitting in the car where Mum should have been. She always picked me up. I thought maybe he was planning a surprise for her. I remember sun and blue sky. I remember the white of the clouds seemed louder than the words when he said them.

He drove home. We sat in the driveway and I wished he would drag out the moment before we went inside, drag it out forever. He unclipped his seat belt and went in the house.

I sat there thinking about this time when Louise had invited most kids to her party but me. On the day she was having it I lay in bed feeling heavy and then this music started up in the living room. I went in and Mum and her friend Celia were playing the Rolling Stones. It was the first time I'd heard them and it felt like that riff was rising from somewhere inside me. Mum and Celia were thrashing around in the music and I thrashed with them. Celia said, "I'm so fucking glad they wrote this song."

And Mum yelled, "I'm so fucking glad they wrote it, too." I stopped dancing. She never swore. "Sometimes you got to let go, Charlie," she shouted, so I did. I shook the world out and shook something else in and I knew then that I had a way to be happy if I needed it.

The day she died I sat in the car till the world got dark. Till I was sure I heard the Stones playing. I ran inside but the only sound was a tap dripping in the laundry.

Dad didn't talk about the accident that night or ever. It was Gran who told me that Mum died crossing a road; a truck driver didn't see the red light and hit her on the way through the intersection. Mum was carrying a set of chef's knives and a book of guitar music. The truck driver was carrying a load from the country. When they got up that morning, neither of them knew where they were headed.

Dad worked a little less after the accident. He hired lots of babysitters and swapped to mostly day shifts, but it didn't make much difference. The house was quiet either way.

Mum and I talk a lot, so it almost feels like she never left me. When I visit the country at Christmas, she comes, too, and she talks more than ever. The thing most people don't know about ghosts is that they travel inside and around you. Mum's in my head and in the water and the rocks and the grass. She tells me how it was when she and Dad fell in love. How it felt when her mum and dad moved overseas and she missed them. How she found it hard to fit in sometimes.

Dad packed up most of the photos of her but I have two. She wrote her name on the back of my favorite one: Arabella Charlotte Webb. Almost like the character from the book. She was sixteen years old, laughing and spinning on an old tire in the river. She was two years away from knowing me. Eleven years away from dead. She was beautiful. A hundred times more beautiful than me.

I keep my second-favorite picture in my sock drawer. I don't look at it very often. It's of Mum and me on a sunny morning. We're out the front of our house, and it's my birthday. She's holding on to the back of my bike. I remember she'd wrapped the whole thing up in colored paper and put it outside my door. It rusted in the shed after she died. I haven't ridden since.

Whenever I tried, Mum's voice purred in the wheels. "Miss me, miss me, miss me," it said. I did. I missed her so much nothing felt right anymore. I feel like we're chasing each other.

I'm chasing her to find the rest of myself and she's chasing me to show me who I was meant to be.

Gran and Mum are the people I talk to the most. The dead are quiet when it comes to secrets. They keep them in a place that no one knows about and no one can find. They know how bad I want to fit in, how bad I want to meet a boy who's not put off by an impromptu roll into the pool or the occasional incident of public nudity.

Some nights I want so bad it's hard to sleep, so I spend the time practicing my guitar. I'm getting really good. Old Gus says, "You're the biz, kid," when I play well in a lesson. He's been saying I'm the biz quite a bit lately. He's been saying, "You could do this for a living." I couldn't, though. Not unless there's a living in singing to the dark.

That's when I sing the best, voice spinning into air, spinning silk around me. While I'm singing like that, people dying doesn't matter quite so much. "Sing it, Charlie," Mum says, and I do. I sing it to the ghosts in my head.

Catacomb Days

The sky's a furry blue blanketing
The crowd at the funeral
Clouds bright
Washing-powder white
The wind smells like roses
And something no one can name
A car backfires, kids run
She's eating tiny sandwiches
Trying to make sense of the sun
And what it thinks it's doing

She's lost in catacomb days

She lets a ghost catch a ride
They crack a few jokes about not being alive
And how the music was deader than the dead
She's thinking words like "dirt bed"
But she doesn't say
Anyway
The ghost's hands are warm
And her dad's hands are clay
The ghost asks what she's thinking
But she can't say

She's lost in catacomb days

She wonders if she'll come back

If no one shows her how

And the ghost looks out the window

Says wow

I'd die for

One more

Taste of cake and bread and wine

Those little sugar biscuits

With real chunks of lemon rind

I'm aching for the day when I was blood

Aching for some hands to rain some skin across my skin

Aching for that moment when I let a person in

Aching just to want again

The ghost asks, "Don't you want to want?"

But she can't say

Maybe one day

For now she's lost in catacomb days

Rose

I ride past Charlie at the gas station and meet Luke and Dave out the front of the milk bar. "We missed the last bus because of you," Luke says, and keeps saying it till I want to glue his stupid mouth shut. "We could be on our way to the movies right now if we'd been a second faster, but no, you had to wave at one last car."

"She gets it, all right?" Dave says, but he's pissed off as well. The best way to spend Sunday is at the movies. How was I to know Mrs. Holly agreed to bring us home if we got ourselves there? "No one said you two had to wait. Could have left for the bus without me."

"Can't even get chips." Luke nods his head at the milk bar. "Shop's closed again. I'm going home. Coming?" he asks me.

"No."

"There aren't any more buses, Rose," he says, and I'm yelling on the inside: Don't you think I know that, Luke? Don't you think I know that every day in this place turns out exactly the same as all the rest?

"There's nothing to wait for," he says. "No buses or cars. Nothing." He shoves the last word in my face.

"See, Luke, now I'm sure there's something to wait for because I've known you for sixteen years and you've never, never been right."

"I'm right this time. You could wait all day and nothing's coming round that corner." He starts reading from the bus timetable. "Ten-fifty. Last bus on a Sunday."

"Shut up."

"Next bus, nine a.m. Monday morning." I kick his knee out from behind him so he bounces forward. "Right, you asked for it," he yells, and I start running a second too late. Dave shakes his head and sits down to watch while Luke grabs my T-shirt and drags me back to the timetable. "Say I'm right." He's shouting and laughing at the same time. "Say it, Rosie. For once say, 'Luke, you are right.'" He holds my shirt tighter and hacks up spit in the back of his throat. "Say it or wear it, Rose. . . ."

Before I give in, I hear wheels on gravel. Luke and I look up as the old blue Ford stops in front of the shop. Charlie stares at us through the window. She hugs her guitar tight. "What were you saying, Luke?" I ask.

"That's not worth waiting for. Just Charlie Dorkin back in

town. Must be summer." He hunches over and brushes his hair forward into his face. "Who am I?" he asks.

I open my mouth to laugh but catch the sound in time and push it back in my throat. "Shut up, Luke." I can't believe I didn't think of it before. Charlie arrives for Christmas every year and leaves two or three weeks later. Mum loves her. She's been on my back for years to make friends with Charlie. The Duskins are probably the only people in the world Mum and Dad might let me go to the city with. I could stay with her. Let's face it, I'd be doing her a favor. I'll probably be the only friend she's ever had.

"Her name's Charlie Duskin," I say.

"What do you care?" Luke asks. "You're the one who said she was weird in the first place."

"That was before."

"Before what?"

"Before I started comparing her to you. Let go of my top, idiot." I push him off and leave both of them at the bus stop. I walk close enough to Charlie on my way past for her to see me smile.

Her eyes always bothered me when we were kids. They still do. They make mine ache trying to see where they end. She used to watch Dave, Luke, and me when she came to visit. Once she spent the whole summer spying on us from her gran's plum tree, staring out from the branches with those shiny possum eyes. She never asked if she could join us; she hid in the leaves and watched, licking juice from her fingers.

"Charlie's lovely, Rose, and all on her own when she comes

down for the summer." Mum said almost the same thing every year.

"She doesn't want to be friends. She spies on us," I answered once. "If I spied on people, you'd kill me. She gets to do whatever she likes. She doesn't have jobs around the house. Nothing."

Charlie would sit next to her dad in the shop and eat whatever she liked and he never told her it was nearly time for dinner. "I'm going to the river," she'd say, and he never hassled her about when she'd be back.

"You'll learn the hard way," Mum said, and I knew I'd gone too far. I didn't mean I wanted Mum to die. I meant Charlie didn't have it as bad as everyone thought she did.

Her gran invited Luke and Dave and me over once a few years back. Mum told me I had to go. She made me wear this dress that itched and shoes that pinched and I was so pissed off that I made Dave and Luke promise not to talk to Charlie when we went inside. I didn't want to be friends with her and no one could make me.

I remember one time when she came to my house. I think it was in Year 7. Her gran had sent her over with a message for Mum. She knocked and Dave, Luke, and I came out of the door. I told her Mum was inside, and the three of us kept walking. Dave hesitated, but he followed in the end. It felt good to leave her on the step. I couldn't stand how desperate she was to be part of us. If she'd told us to piss off, maybe I would have liked her more.

She doesn't spy now. She walks around town looking like

this is the last place in the world she wants to be. Maybe she and I actually have something in common.

Maybe we can use each other to get what we want this summer. I'll give her a bit of what she's been staring at all these years and she can take me with her when she goes. I'd do anything to get to the city. Even hang out with Charlie Duskin.

Charlie

Rose Butler gives the death stare as we pull into town. "Your friends seem glad to have you back, Charlotte," Dad says. He thinks Louise is my friend, too. It's hard to believe the restaurant reviewers say he's got an eye for detail. The man misses everything.

He wears these 1950s glasses, tiny squares that look cool but don't do much. I tried them on once and the world got soft and lost its edges. "You drive with these things on?" I asked, looking at someone who could have been Dad or King Kong or the coatrack as it turned out. "You'll inherit my sight, Charlotte," he said, taking them off me without cracking a smile. "Let's laugh together then."

Rose has gone inside by the time I grab my last bag from the car and put it on the step outside the shop with the others. Luke and Dave don't take long to follow. The street's empty as I turn the door handle and bang my shoulder against glass. "It's locked. Doesn't he know we're coming?"

"Sit down a minute," Dad says, and I know he's not happy about something because his head tilts the smallest bit to the side instead of staying straight on.

"Grandpa's okay, isn't he?"

The door behind us opens before he answers. "Come in, come in," Grandpa says, and his voice is grass-dry. I lean close to kiss his cheek. He smells like he's taken a bath in soup and toasted sandwiches and the toilet. The inside of the house doesn't smell any better. Food's running low. The place is dusty. I spend the afternoon cleaning while Grandpa sleeps and Dad writes orders for the shop.

At about six, Dad wakes Grandpa and cooks some scrambled eggs. We eat listening to Rose's family having a barbecue next door. Grandpa goes to bed early. Dad goes for a walk.

I go outside and play my guitar quietly so the Butlers can't hear me. "I'd like to welcome everybody here tonight; this first song is for my gran and grandpa." I drag out the chords and slow the tempo of "Smashed-Up World."

Gran was always at me to sing for people. She wanted me to go in this talent quest they hold here every January. I imagined playing in it and that was as close as I got. In my imagining, I'm onstage, singing an upbeat song to a crowd that can't wait to applaud.

I don't play upbeat tonight. I strum "A Little Wanting Song." E-flat. Low and hollow. Soft and sad. I let the old voice of the guitar rise like the moon and it floats and dips around me.

A Little Wanting Song

It's just a little wanting song

It won't go on for all that long

Just long enough to say

How much I'm wishing for

Just a little more

Rose

"Hang out the washing for me?" Mum asks when I walk in the door. She doesn't ask me where I was this morning or why I was up so early. She doesn't say anything except "Remember to take the clothes in if it rains, love. I'm on the afternoon shift at the caravan park."

She never used to worry about the washing in a storm. She went outside and danced around. Now she worries about balancing the books or if the workers are cleaning the vans properly.

I can't imagine her doing it at all anymore, let alone doing it in a car with Dad. I guess everyone's got secrets. I told Luke and Dave about Mum getting pregnant before she was married. They looked at me, burgers halfway to their mouths. "Unbelievable," Luke said. "They did it in a car?"

"What sort of car was it?" Dave asked.

"A Holden."

"That's a good car, Rosie," he said through a mouthful of food.

The only thing that mattered to Dave was that they did it in a great car. The only thing that mattered to Luke was that they did it at all. My best friends have their secrets written on T-shirts.

It doesn't take long for them to walk into my backyard today. I try to leave them behind, but they always follow me. "Dave, get my mum's bra off your head. Either help or get lost."

"Stop messing around, dickhead, or we'll never get out of here," Luke says, and throws a peg at him.

I've known Dave so long that I can tell what he's going to do before he does it. I don't want to meet the person who can predict what Luke's about to do; they'd have to be crazier than him.

We were all born in the same hospital. I came first, then Luke. "Dave took bloody ages," his mum says, and winks. She only swears when she talks about giving birth to him. "Twenty-four bloody hours," she says, and pulls Dave in close. He just acts like he's annoyed. His dad's the one he fights with.

Mr. Robbie's given Dave a hard time for as long as I can remember, like when he made him sign up for the local footy team. Most boys in town are in it; there's nothing else to do on Saturdays in winter. Most guys weren't as small as Dave was in Year 7, though. Coach only let him on the ground because his older brother used to play. Mr. Robbie played, too. Years ago. No one asked Dave what he wanted.

I walked up to the wire fence before his first match and stood as close to him as I could. "You'll be all right," I said. Sometimes a friend doesn't need the truth.

Mr. Robbie didn't make a sound as Dave fell the first time. He watched his son moving like a scared rabbit running wild and barely blinked. My breath ran crazy with Dave as he zigzagged across the field. He didn't see Luke grab the ball and swing back with his boot. He got in the way, and Luke kicked him instead, thumped him right between the legs. Luke was really, really good at footy; his boot connected with Dave so hard he almost sent him sailing through the posts. Every boy on the field closed his legs in sympathy. The rest of us closed our eyes.

"For God's sake, get up," his dad called out after a bit. I would have loved to test how quickly Mr. Robbie'd get up if I walked over and slammed *him* in the nuts.

At the end of the game Dave and his dad got into the car without saying a word. I would have cried that day, seeing him drive off, except I kept imagining Mrs. Robbie waiting behind the wire door.

Luke and I sat by the river for hours after the match. "I didn't mean it," he kept saying, and I felt like I was the one who'd kicked Dave and been kicked, all at the same time. I hate that feeling, worrying about them.

When Dave's dad gives him a hard time, he goes wandering round the town at night. I see him, scuffing at the dirt, his arms wrapped tight round himself, like if he lets go he'll fall apart. He doesn't want to talk. Luke and I tried once, and he told us to piss off.

Lately I worry about Dave a lot, because every time Luke gets in trouble, Dave gets in even more trying to help him. It used to be that Luke only hung out with us and that kept him kind of safe. But last year I started babysitting, and Dave got a summer job at the garage. That meant Luke had time on his hands.

He started spending it with Antony Barellan. There are two sides of town, and the Barellan kids hang out on the wrong one. They sit outside the fish-and-chips shop near the turnoff to Henderson's Road. They don't wait for something to happen. They wait to happen to something.

The day Luke got arrested, Dave and I were working. I heard the siren screaming across town from my place. The other kids with Luke were smart enough to run.

Dave and I huddled outside the police station. It got colder and colder and later and later, but neither of us talked about leaving. We found out afterward that they were only keeping Luke to give him a scare. We didn't know that then, though, and all night we thought about losing him. "How come he does dumb stuff all the time?" I asked while we waited.

"He's there at the wrong time, and the wrong thing's happening, and he thinks, Why not?"'

"So what you're saying is my boyfriend's an idiot?"

I never mind when Dave says stuff like that about Luke. I figure he's earned the right to, maybe even more than I have.

"How come you never do stupid stuff except with him?" I asked that night.

"My old man would kill me, Rosie. Even I'm smart enough to work that one out."

Dave talks about himself like that all the time. He's not dumb, though. He can take a car apart and put it back together in under an hour. "It doesn't take a genius to do that, Rosie."

"Not everyone who's knocked down in their first footy game gets back up and goes in again," I said to him once.

"Most kids in this town don't get knocked down to start with."

I held Dave's hand outside the police station. He acts like he doesn't need anyone but he's looking for someone as much as anyone else; he just doesn't know how to say it.

Nights like that one make me realize how much I'll miss Dave and Luke when I go. I think how easy it would be to stay. Dad would love it if I studied by correspondence or went to college in the next big town and worked part-time at the caravan park with Mum.

But then I think about spending my whole life with boys who read car magazines and think "amoeba" is the name of a band. I think about spending my life sitting on plastic chairs waiting for fish and chips to arrive. That sort of thinking can kill a person.

So instead I think, Get out, Rose, get out. See nights that last forever in Antarctica. See where the world began.

Today I feel like I am seeing where the world began, right here in my backyard. Dave's running around like a strange dinosaur with my mum's bra making two huge ears on his head. Luke chases him, trips him up, and sits on his stomach.

"Got him, Rose. What do you want to do with him?"

"With Dave?" I laugh. "Nothing. Absolutely nothing."

He grabs at Luke's ankles then and they tumble over dirt, shouting at each other so loud the whole town can hear. "Bloody get off, Luke," Dave yells. "I've got a prickle in my jocks!"

Luke pulls Dave's jeans down fast. "That better? God, Dave, what girl'll ever go out with you in undies like those?"

"If you plan on stuffing around all afternoon, then leave, will you? I've got things to do."

"Get out of the way, Dave." Luke picks himself up off the ground. "She's gone from Rosie to bitch in less than six seconds."

"Better watch out, then," I say, and chase him. I run till I'm out of breath and the clouds spin above me when I fall. The three of us lounge together under the shade of the huge old tree that's been here as long as us. "What things other than this have you got to do, Rosie?" Dave asks.

"She's got nothing." Luke laughs.

"Well, you got less than nothing," I say, and point at his open fly. The clouds slow to drifting above us.

Charlie

I'm sitting on a crate behind the counter having a break when Rose and Luke walk into the shop this afternoon. Dad's in the kitchen drinking his coffee. We've been up since six cleaning the place.

They can't see me but I can see them. I don't stand because I've been standing all morning. Plus, this is my small protest against Luke and Rose. I can't serve you if I don't exist. Get lost in that existential dilemma.

It's too late to stand by the time Dave walks in, so I sit eating my Mars bar and listening. "About time this place opened again," Luke says. "Lazy-arse old man should sell the shop if he doesn't want to work."

"Lazy-arse old man just lost his wife," Dave says. "So give it a rest."

I've thought it before and I'll think it again. Dave is a guy worth writing songs about.

"We should steal stuff while he's not here," Luke says.

Luke is also a guy worth writing songs about, but a different kind of song. He rings the bell on the counter over and over. I finish my Mars bar. Dad walks out of the kitchen, flicks his eyes at me, and then looks back at Luke. "Is there some kind of fast-food emergency?" he asks in the voice that he uses when he's being funny, which is pretty much the same voice he uses when he's not being funny.

"Yeah," Luke says. "We need three lots of chips. Three burgers, no beetroot. Three Cokes."

They go outside. Dad and I go into the kitchen. He doesn't say anything about me hiding on the floor. Just pulls out meat and buns and chips and eggs and lettuce and beetroot.

"They don't want beetroot."

"They don't know what they're missing," he says, and it makes me think of this time in Year 6 when he cooked his special burgers for Dahlia and me. We'd been in a fight with some kids who hung out on the corner near the end of my street. They called us ugly names as we walked past, but Dahlia wouldn't take the shortcut so we could avoid them. "They don't own the street, Charlie."

That day on our way past, one of the older kids sung the word "loser" at us. "Dickhead!" Dahlia yelled. She ran after them, shouting more names while I watched from the end of the street.

"Why'd you let them call us that?" she asked when they'd gone. "You should tell them to shove it up their butts." She looked so serious, and I tried to look serious back, but I kept thinking that "butt" is a funny word. I started laughing and then she started and we couldn't stop. Every time we got our breath one of us would say, "Shove it up their butts. Shove it up their butts," and start the whole thing rolling again.

I made up this song on the guitar, which was basically just one line—"Tell them to shove it up their butts"—with a little harmonizing. Dahlia was belting out, "Shove, shove, shove it up their butts, butts, bu—" when Dad walked in.

"Hello, Dahlia, Charlotte. Can I ask to whom this song is dedicated?"

"Some boys down the road called us losers, Mr. Duskin."

He put his hands in his pockets and took them out. Looked at them and didn't find the answer written there, so he made us two of his special burgers. "The secret is the beetroot," he said. "Nobody liked it when I first started making them. Now everybody wants beetroot."

"You're right," Dahlia said after she finished. "It's different, but it's good."

That night, just before I fell asleep, I felt Dad kiss me so soft I thought maybe I was dreaming. "Being different is the only way to live," he said. I opened my eyes and he was gone.

"Take these orders out for me please, Charlotte?" Dad asks today when he's finished. Mum's somewhere humming that song Dahlia and I wrote. I'm humming it with her as I open the door.

"There's beetroot in this," Luke says after I put his burger on the table in front of him. "I hate beetroot." He lifts the top off the bun and sniffs it.

"I can get you another one," I say.

"I've already been waiting half an hour."

I stand there while Luke slowly spins every piece of beetroot from his burger onto the ground at my feet. A bird comes along but doesn't peck at it. "See," he says. "Birds don't even like that shit."

You didn't even try it, I think. "Shove it up your butt." Shit. I didn't mean to say that out loud.

"What did you say?" Luke asks, pushing his burger to the side.

Dave laughs. "She said shove it up your butt, mate."

"Shove it up your own butt," Luke says to him.

"Funnily enough, I don't feel like doing that."

Luke gets madder and starts going on about how I'm a waitress and how the customer is always right while Rose stares at me like any minute she'll slap me from here to the other end of the street.

"Shut up, Luke," she says instead. "Charlie said you could have another one." Then she smiles, which makes me think her plan for revenge might be more involved than a simple slapping. "Are you working here all day?" she asks.

"No."

Rose Butler's more predictable than Wham! lyrics. Any

minute now she'll say something like "You should work here all day. There's nothing else for you to do."

"Why don't you come down to the river with us after you finish?" she asks. Luke looks at her like she's talking to a pet dog and expecting it to answer back. Dave's mouth hangs open for a bit and then shifts gear into a smile. I'm thinking back over Wham!'s greatest hits.

"Charlie?" she says.

"Maybe." I clear rubbish from the table next to them before I go inside. Dave says to Luke, "Stop complaining. One day you'll work out the beetroot's the best part." Dave saying that doesn't surprise me. The thing that does is hearing Rose agree. I watch them through the window, with my iPod turned up loud.

Rose

"Why'd you invite her?" Luke asks for the fiftieth time on the way down to the river, like asking me over and over will make me change my mind.

"She doesn't know anyone in this place."

"She never has. You weren't nice before."

"Maybe I feel sorry for her. Anyway, it might be fun to hang out with someone new."

"New girls are trouble."

"Luke, you talk to two girls. One's me and one's your mother."

"What's your point?"

"My point is, shut up and be nice to Charlie or you'll only

be talking to one." I don't have to say anything else because he sees the river and sprints toward it.

"So how come you really invited her?" Dave asks.

"I don't know. She might be fun. Maybe she'd be a good girlfriend for you."

"Rose, her gran died this year. Don't make fun of her."

"Maybe I'm bored with you and Luke."

"You've been bored with us before. You never talked to Charlie."

"I only asked her to go swimming. She must get lonely."

"I reckon she must," he says. "I have to get my stuff. Meet you down there."

Dave's felt sorry for Charlie ever since we were kids. Whenever I'd call her Charlie Dorkin, he'd look at the ground till I stopped. He's like that in everything. When we go fishing with Dad, he never keeps what he catches. "Too small," he says when I see him throwing his fish back into the river. They're usually twice as big as his hands.

I feel sorry for Charlie, too. That's why this is good for her. She'll hang out with us for a while, and then she'll have a friend to go back to the city with. I bet I'll be the only one she'll have there. When she rolls out at the end of summer, I'm rolling with her, Dave. Let's face it: I'm doing her a favor.

It's a perfect plan. Charlie Duskin. Even her name sounds like the end of a long, hot day and the beginning of night.

Charlie

I ask Dad if I can finish for the day and he looks up from the accounts he's trying to balance. "I thought you left hours ago," he says, and goes back to the books. I ring the bell three times on the way out the door and wait long enough to hear him shuffling toward it. Maybe I should buy myself a bell.

I don't grab my bathing suit and run to meet Rose. I'm not planning on joining them, on account of how I think it's a plot to kill me. I head for the river, but far away from where they'll be swimming. I head to Mum's place.

She says I should go meet the three of them. She says I'm being dramatic, and I say, "If I am, you're where I got it from." Mum knows I'm thinking of a time our school ran this big fund-raiser. Every class had to do something and ours decided to hold a concert where the parents or the grandparents performed and the kids came to watch. Dad kept saying he'd pay money not to be in the concert but Mum wouldn't let him off the hook. I didn't want him onstage, either. Dad couldn't sing or dance and Mum had this duet planned for their act.

They got up there and the music started and Dad froze. His face didn't even move. Mum looked at him and all the kids were looking, too, and I felt sick. And then she started up. She was Diana Ross dancing around one scared-shitless Supreme and she was moving enough for both of them. She acted like Dad was meant to be standing completely still. When it was his turn to sing, she opened his mouth and sang in a deep voice and the kids thought it was the funniest thing they'd ever seen. Even Louise was laughing.

We're laughing today as we walk along the edge of the water. Mum's pointing out things she remembers and I'm imagining what it would have been like for her growing up in this town. Imagining how she came to be that person who could get onstage and not care what anyone thought.

"Your dad asked me to marry him here," she says like she always does. "He was romantic. Of course, when we were kids, he held my head under the water and nearly drowned me, too."

"Love's kind of weird," I say, and we think about that for a bit.

After a while I feel like swimming and I don't care that I don't have my bathing suit. Everyone swims closer to town, so no one sees me here. I wade into the middle of the stream and let the river take hold of my shirt and swirl it round like

I'm dancing. I sink a little, jeans heavy with water, and the river covers my ears, turning sound to vibration. I keep my eyes closed and imagine that the water rings spinning out come from Mum's old tire, and that the birds in the background are the same ones that flew over her years ago. I imagine I hear her laughing.

Maybe after the picture of Mum in the tire was taken, she lay on the grass, too, her curls pointing crazily in all directions. I climb back up the bank and lie on the ground and the light sings a lullaby, so I close my eyes. Maybe somewhere inside there's a part of me that's as beautiful as she was.

And maybe not.

"Why are you swimming in jeans?" Dave Robbie stands over me, taking in my messy hair and soaking clothes. Unexpected, sure. But not entirely unfixable with a smart comeback. "Because I'm swimming in jeans." Unfortunately, I don't have a smart comeback.

He laughs. "Fair enough. We're further up the river." I follow him because I can't think of an excuse before he says, "You should take off your jeans."

This moment was more romantic when I imagined it. "Sorry?"

"Don't you have your bathing suit on underneath?"

"No."

He nods and we keep walking. It's not like I don't have words in my head. I'm good with words. I'm great. On my own. In the dark. They come flooding. Sometimes I can't sleep I'm swimming in so many words.

It's when I'm around some people that my entire vocabulary goes on vacation. Like now, when Dave's walking next to me wearing an old black singlet and board shorts and the tattoo of a bird on his wrist, every single word in my head except "no" and "huh" is lying somewhere on a beach getting a suntan.

"You want to go home and get your bathing suit?" Dave asks.

Yes. Because that worked out so well before. "No."

"You're kind of weird sometimes. Good weird," he adds quick.

"There's good weird?" I ask. "A whole new world's opening up."

He laughs, and something shifts. Like it did at the start of that party. I don't know what it is, and I don't question it. "I wasn't planning on swimming. It was a spur-of-the-moment kind of thing."

"I swim in my jocks when I have that spur-of-the-moment feeling," Dave says. "You probably wouldn't swim in your jocks."

"Not since I was about five."

We head closer to town. I think about the direction Dave was walking when he found me, and it doesn't make sense. "What were you doing so far up the river?" I ask. He shrugs and grins and rips off a piece of grass for me to keep the flies off my back. "I always see you swimming there," he says. "How come?"

"Just because," I say, wondering when he's seen me before.

Sounds I never heard from insects I can't name flick around us, and my words go vacationing again.

"'Jocks' is a funny word, isn't it?" Dave asks after a while.

"It is," I say, and we have a little laugh.

"Look who I found," Dave says to Rose, and she smiles at me again. He dives into the water and Luke swings over him from a rope tied to a tree at the edge. The whole place echoes as he crashes through the surface and disappears.

Rose fishes under the water for him. "Luke?" she calls. "Luke, stop messing about." He explodes up beside her, laughter bouncing off the hills as he jumps on her back and tries to push her under. She screams and splashes at him with her feet. I soak it all in. Sun. Laughter. Dave.

I can't take my eyes off Luke, running across the grass calling Rose's name. I wonder what "Charlie" might sound like in someone's mouth, shouted out across the day and echoing off mountains.

"Charlie, we're watching DVDs at my place tomorrow night. Want to come?" Rose hovers at the edge of the river before she dives. Water drips down her shoulders.

Luke sneaks up behind her and mouths to me, "Should I push her?" She moves her head the slightest bit toward him, asking me if he's there. I give a nod and she moves to the side. Luke splashes into the cold instead of her. She claps and shakes her hair; tiny tears flick out and disappear into air.

I take some time to think about the DVD night. On the one hand, it means more time with Dave. On the other hand, there's a burning question that's begging to be asked. Why would Luke and Rose suddenly become my welcoming committee? Dahlia always told me I was funny. "Louise'll love you once she knows you." I still haven't said anything that's made her smile. Lucky I didn't hold my breath.

Dave lies beside me to dry off, and he smells like car oil and grass and sunscreen. He laughs at Rose and Luke for a while, then he turns to me. " 'Beetle' is a weird word, too." He picks one off my arm. "It's a diving beetle. Stays under the water for ages. Holds spare air under its wings." There's one on his arm but I leave it where it is.

We stay at the river for hours. The afternoon is warm and my skin is cold and my stomach is rumbling. Night is nearly here and the light is the color of a sweet yellow pear.

Rose and I leave Dave and Luke at the end of the road that leads to their houses and turn off toward our street. "So you'll come to watch DVDs tomorrow?" she asks as we reach the gate of her house. I see the branches of the plum tree sticking out over the back fence. I remember Dave lying next to me. I hear Mum telling me to take a chance. "Yeah. Okay. I'll come."

The yellow light stops at my door. The curtains are drawn, and the living room is dark. Gran squeezed every last second out of the day when she was alive, like juice from a bright, shiny lemon. She always tossed her hat off when she worked in the garden. "Stupid thing keeps slipping," she'd say. "You keep yours on, Charlie Brown; you'll have skin that looks like a join-the-dot picture." She couldn't stand having the curtains closed before nightfall. "House is like a funeral parlor," she said once when Grandpa closed them too early. Dad cleared his throat and looked at me.

I heard them arguing about it later. "You think she doesn't know her mother's dead, Joe?" Gran asked. "I wonder if you know sometimes."

"It's none of your business."

"Maybe you're right. But it's hers. It's not doing either of you any good, living like this."

"Enough!" Dad yelled silence into the air. I've never heard him loud like that before. I've tried hard since then not to talk about Mum.

"Grandpa?" I call.

"Outside, Charlie."

The garden was always Gran's place. It feels like any minute she'll shuffle round the corner and call to us like she used to. "Albert, Charlie, we've got a lemon on the tree." Her voice mixed with the sound of insects, rising in the dropping light.

I remember this path she made me once. "It'll lead you somewhere special," she said. It twisted round the outside of her plants, then curled in toward the middle of her garden. It took me past the vegetable patch and her chicken coop, down to the back of the yard. I saw two of the most beautiful flowers, bright splashes of red against green. I leaned in and smelled them, but they were empty, like a film with the sound turned down.

"Charlie," Gran said, walking up behind me, "they're not what I wanted you to see." She pointed out over the back fence at huge mountains, singing purple and blue in the distance. "Beautiful, aren't they?" she asked, and I nodded, but I kept thinking about those bright, silent flowers.

Looking at Grandpa's eyes tonight, I know he's not seeing the mountains. The path's too overgrown. We sit together for a while, staring at the tangle. He's thinking about Gran, and I am, too. But the river keeps creeping in. I've got the start of a song in my head that's warm and full of light. Spattered with chords that move like water.

Rose

I'm taking out the rubbish around nine tonight when I see Dave walking past on the other side of the road, arms wrapped around himself, face telling the world to piss off. I call to Mum I'll be back soon and follow him.

He's staring at the footy oval when I catch up, sitting on the bench under the one light the club leaves on to stop people vandalizing. "You following me?" he asks.

"No," I say. "I come here all the time, late at night, to hang out on my own."

"Thought you were bored with me and Luke."

"Not a lot else on offer."

"Except Charlie," he says.

"If you like her so much, get on with it and ask her out. She'd say yes in a second."

Luke and I give Dave shit about not having a girlfriend, but the truth is Dave could have anyone he wants. He just hasn't wanted anyone so far. He came back from the Year 8 holidays and all the girls in our class started laughing with him instead of at him.

They were laughing when he wasn't even funny. They stared at him on the way past. At his arms sticking out of his ripped-off black singlet. At his eyes, half hiding under his hair. They gave up their spot in the line for the school canteen. "Unheard of," Luke said when a little space cleared for him and Dave. "You see that, Rosie? Girls love us."

"It's not you. It's Dave."

"Dave?" Dave asked.

"Yeah, dickhead," I said. "You."

I'd worked it out the week before when Justine Morenci walked past the three of us having lunch and her head did this three-sixty-degree spin. Justine Morenci is a ten on a scale of five. You don't get on her radar unless you've made it. Dave had done what most guys only dream about: he'd found a way of changing his molecular structure and reversing the gene that makes him invisible to girls like Justine. And what do you think Dave does with this amazing molecular evolution? Nothing. He spends his weekends at the garage, working on cars.

Justine cornered me in the toilets after a few weeks of attempted Dave pickup. I think she was going through some molecular transformation herself. Dave must have been the first guy who looked straight through her. "So, Rose, I'm planning on asking Dave to the school social. Think he'll be interested?"

"Sure," I said, and she smiled. "If you grow four wheels and get some license plates, he'll be all over you."

She asked and Dave went along because he didn't know how to turn her down. He stood at the side of the room, and when she said they should go out the back, he ran away faster than those cars he spends so much time on.

"Did you hear me, Dave?" I ask. "Make a move on Charlie."

"You think she'd go out with anyone because she's not like you. She's gorgeous. Fucking gorgeous. You've spent too long in this place to see."

"I don't think anyone can have her," I say after a while, because it feels wrong to sit next to Dave and not talk.

"This town," he says, and throws a rock at the light and knocks it out.

Charlie

Gus says when he met Beth he heard drums everywhere. "Drums in my blood. Drums in my sleep. Kid, when I met Beth, the air drummed."

"We met at a rock concert," she told me later. "The air actually was drumming."

Nina Simone's playing in the background today, but she's not what's putting jazz in my blood. It's the thought of seeing Dave tonight. I've got little skipping beats in me. Whenever I check the clock, it's ticking backward. Rose finally walks in at four. I grab snacks from the shelves. "You're so lucky," she says. "Your dad lets you do anything."

"I'm so lucky I can hardly stand it," I say, and ring the bell a couple of times on the way out the door.

I follow Rose and it occurs to me that the answer to my burning question might be in my arms. She and Luke want to hang out with me because I'm a ticket to free food.

"Ever notice it's impossible to walk straight when you're trying?" Rose asks on the way to her place, holding her arms out. Her feet topple into the grass but she catches herself easily.

"Dad took me to a circus once and the tightrope guy walked blindfolded from one side of the room to the other," I say.

"Did he have a net?"

"Just a thread of steel to balance on."

It was the first circus I'd been to since Mum died. Dad and I saw loads of things, but it was that guy I dreamed about. He swayed on the wire in my dream, and once he fell he became me, grabbing at huge handfuls of air.

"It's all in their minds, isn't it?" Rose asks. "They don't fall because they imagine they won't. You try it. Close your eyes and walk."

I watch Rose feel her way along the edge of the grass with her toes. I pretend to do the same but I keep my eyes open half a moon. She's got nothing in her arms and I'm carrying stuff so I can't use mine for balance.

"Sometimes I'd rather be at school than on holidays," Rose says, eyes still closed. "What's your school like?"

"It's okay."

"More than okay, I bet. There must be loads of clubs and excursions. Are you in the band?"

"I'm in the big choir. I'm this little dot way up in the back."

I can sing in front of people like that. I sink into the music and disappear. Dahlia wanted me to play my guitar and sing solo at the final school concert this year. It's a big deal, and you have to audition in November to get a spot, and then the show's on in the last week of school. "You could perform one of your songs," she said.

"It's not my thing," I told her. I could sing in the shower, sure. I could play songs in front of her, too. But performing to a crowd? I could already taste that crumbling song.

"It is your thing," Dahlia said. "It's exactly your thing, only no one knows it. You're always saying people don't like you but people can't like something that's not there."

"What are you thinking about?" Rose asks, staring at me.

I didn't realize she'd opened her eyes. "I'm thinking I'm hungry."

"Yeah," she says. "I'm hungry, too. But there's nothing to eat at home."

I hold up the snacks.

"It's a good thing you came to town." She smiles.

Mrs. Butler's on the way out as we're walking in. She pushes a basket of washing toward Rose. "Put these on the line for me, love. Could you look after your cousins? I have to work late, and your dad's sleeping."

"Luke and Dave are coming over."

"They can come tomorrow. Jenny's sick. I have to do her shift."

Rose calls Luke. "Mum says I have to do housework. You

can't come over." She hangs up, grabs the washing, and slams the back door.

"Nice to see you, Charlie," Mrs. Butler says, and slams the front door.

"Nice to see you, too."

Rose's yard looks different from the ground. The last time I sat in Gran's plum tree all those summers ago, Rose was alone, lying in the yard. Every now and then she'd roll over onto her back, slowly baking herself in the sun. That was the day I stopped hoping she'd invite me over. It was clear she didn't need anyone. "You don't have to help," she says. "Go watch the movie at Luke's place with Dave."

I peg washing on the line.

"At least falling off a tightrope would be exciting," she says.

"For a second, I guess. Before the crushing pain." I hang things carefully so they don't come undone in the wind.

"Crushing pain's better than crushing boredom." She stabs her mum's jeans with the pegs and slaps at the legs. "Don't you ever feel like doing something different from what you do every day?"

"All the time," I tell her, but she's not listening. She's talking without taking a breath. "I call this Mum's scuba suit," she says, holding up underwear. "She gets pissed and tells me I'll know all about being old one day. Even when I'm old, I won't wear that."

Pegs fall. She leaves them on the ground and pulls more from the basket. "I bet you're glad you don't have to cook for your cousins. Bet you're thinking, Thank God I don't have to hang out my mum's underwear. Thank God my mum doesn't make me hang out washing from the caravan park. Thank God my mum doesn't make me stay at home while she's out working." She steps on a peg and cracks its back.

I peg a towel so it hangs between us but her voice keeps going in the background. "It's like I talk and she doesn't hear," Rose says.

I peg another towel.

"It's like she's not even there."

And another.

"Like . . ." She stops, and what she's said catches up with her. A yappy dog barks from a yard down the street. We finish hanging the washing in silence. I walk out from behind my towel fence and pick up the fallen pegs. "I might go home now."

"No, wait. Stay. I'll cook you dinner."

"Why?" I ask.

The shadow of a bird passes over her face. "People change," she says. I'm not sure whether she means me or her. I hang around for dinner either way.

Rose turns on the TV for her cousins. I look through her CD collection while she's cooking. I don't have a problem talking to Gus or Beth or the customers at the music shop because we're talking about things I know. People say, "There's this song by a girl and it goes kind of like this."

I listen and say, "Yeah, that sounds like Luscious Jackson," and I find it for them. I pull out a few other things I know they'll like and I get a kick out of watching while they listen.

They're thinking, This track is my life. Exactly. The music kicks in and maybe the bad times kick out and maybe the world's a little better for them than it was before. After they've gone, Gus says, "You're the biz, kid." But I didn't find them music for the money and he knows it.

Rose has mostly chart stuff in her collection, the kind Dahlia likes. It's all fast beats and boppy. I'm not against the boppy beat, but there's better boppy beats out there. There are songs that swing a person out of themselves for a while.

"Dinner's ready," Rose calls, and we sit down to burned chops and lumpy potatoes. "God, this is disgusting. Sorry," she says, spitting some out.

"You know, I'm really good at making toast because my dad's a chef."

"Toast sounds good," she says, staring at something that might have been a chop in another life if she hadn't burned it beyond all recognition. "Toast sounds really good."

While I'm spreading butter, I think about how I like the noise in Rose's house, lines of music, threaded and knotted over the top of one another. Knives hitting plates, chairs scraping floor, kids screaming, her dad's slippers shuffling his solo, "Can't a Man Get Any Sleep Around Here?" Mixed together it sounds like a little kitchen symphony.

Mr. Butler takes over babysitting, and we sit in Rose's room. She's got this picture on her wall of tiny churches and dollhouses floating in a dark ocean. "They're protistan shells," she says. "Made of silica and lime. We learned about them in science."

Before today, I never imagined Rose would be the sort of

girl to care about school. I imagined her to be the sort to hang around the back sheds, smoking. I guess you have to listen to a person to really know them. "What are protistans?" I ask.

"They're these tiny organisms that live in the ocean. You can't see them unless they're magnified about two thousand times. People look right through them," she says. "It seems like such a waste for things like that to be invisible."

I look closely at the floating glass houses. "I hear my old music box when I look at them," I say before I think that it might sound stupid.

"When I was a kid," she tells me, "I wanted to know how someone trapped music in that tiny space. I smashed it to see. You ever do that?"

I shake my head. Mum gave me that music box.

"What's it like living in the city?" she asks. "What do you do when you're not at school?"

"I play guitar and write songs. I work at a music store on Acland Street, down on the beach. It's close to where I live, close to loads of places to eat. Luna Park's near the water. From the Ferris wheel, Mum and I used to look over the ocean on one side and the city on the other."

"I've never been to the ocean. I want to go there. Go to the city. Go somewhere that leads places."

"The river leads somewhere," I say.

"Yeah, but I can't see further than the bend."

Gran used to tell me where the river went. She described the way one small trickle met up with another, how eventually you're at a roaring mouth. She loved to talk about where she and Grandpa had traveled before Dad was born. "My gran's been heaps of places. She said this town was as beautiful as any she'd seen."

"Yeah, but she got to see all the others."

"You'll see them," I say.

"How do you know?"

I look at her poster and think about it. "Because you want to."

Down the hall, one of her cousins cries. "I can't stand kids screaming," Rose says.

I plug my iPod into her computer and play a different mix than the one in her kitchen. I play some stuff to make her feel like she's someplace else, someplace better.

A minute into Moloko and Rose is up and dancing. Apart from Mum and occasionally Dahlia, I never dance in front of other people on account of me being so shit at it. But I watch Rose jumping around and she doesn't look all that much better than me. She looks kind of like Dahlia does when she bounces on my bed. "You got to cut loose once in a while," Mum says. Five minutes into Moloko and I'm on the bedroom dance floor with Rose. I'm someplace else, someplace better.

Rose

I dance to Charlie's music, spin and spin and forget about my cousin screaming and my mum pissing me off and how sick I am of this town. She loads songs onto my laptop and I need her to be like that, to want to be my friend, but I'm thinking at the same time, Why would you do that? Why give yourself away to someone who said the things I did in the backyard this afternoon? I said them by accident; I didn't mean to hurt her, but I still said them.

"This song was my gran's favorite," she tells me, and I'm expecting some old guy to come on but instead "I'm gonna smash up the world" screams from the speakers. "We didn't play it at the funeral," Charlie says, and almost laughs.

I wouldn't go to her gran's funeral and it was practically

next door. "I barely know the Duskins," I'd told Mum when she asked, and it's the first thing she didn't push me on. I guess she figured she couldn't make me care. Dave went with his parents and I gave him shit about wearing a suit.

Charlie and her dad stayed for about a week. Dave and I were sitting at the bus stop when they left. We weren't waiting for anything; we were filling in time. She kissed her grandpa goodbye. He barely kissed her back. I looked at Dave to say something, but he was staring at his shoes. "Let's find Luke," he said, and took off ahead of me up the street.

Old Mr. Duskin still ran the shop after that, but there wasn't much you could buy in the place. Mum sent me in for things like cans of tomatoes and pineapple that we didn't even need. I started sneaking into the supermarket when Mum sent me for things. The only time I went back into the Duskins' shop was when Dave wanted something. "You can get that at the supermarket," I told him.

"I know," he said, and went inside to buy it from Charlie's grandpa.

"Thanks," I say before Charlie goes. "For the music. For hanging out."

She acts like it's no big deal. "I'll burn you some more stuff," she says.

"You should bring your guitar next time. Sing me some of your songs."

"Nah. They're just things I write to make me and Dahlia, my best friend, laugh."

"If Dahlia laughs, then I probably will."

"Dahlia's not hard to make laugh," she says. "She still cracks up when you say 'butt' to her."

I think Charlie might be lying. I don't think she plays at all. "Well, I'll listen when you feel like it."

After she's gone, I play the music she left me. I watch the tiny protistan shells, and I think about her telling me I'll leave here. The light makes them look like old blue Fords and guitars drifting through the ocean. The last song on my laptop is about a night with no moon. The singer's voice is velvet and sad. "Silver dots in darkness," she sings. "She's miles away from morning. Midnight blood is thick with longing."

I drift, almost sleeping, and the voice drifts around me. A thought about silkworms drifts as well. Mum bought me some a long time ago. They spin silk inside the cocoon, but to get at it you have to boil them alive before they hatch. One of my teachers told me and I came home and asked Mum if it was true. She nodded. "But we just won't use them for silk," she said. "We'll keep them as pets; that's all." I ran my hand over the rough cocoon. I wanted so bad to see the silk.

The singer spins the chorus one last time.

Charlie

Sunny notes from an open window wake me Christmas Eve. That and a couple of dead women yelling at me to get Grandpa and go pick out a tree.

That's not so easy. Mostly he sleeps till late afternoon. He gets up and sleeps some more in front of the television. The curtains stay closed, and the light from the box throws this eerie blue glow over him. If I wrote a sound track to the life we're living now, it would be a slow note echoing from a saxophone.

He's asleep when I look into his room late this morning. I shake his shoulder but he doesn't wake up, so I get close to his face and check that he's breathing.

"Is there something you want, Charlie?"

"Shit, Grandpa. You nearly gave me a heart attack."

"It's strange, but that's almost exactly what I was about to say. What is it?"

Now that I've woken him, it doesn't seem so important. "It's Christmas tree time."

"There's an old plastic one in the cupboard under the stairs. We'll use that this year." He closes his eyes, and that dusty note rises again.

I let him sleep. I know a few things about ghosts. The only way to stop them getting inside you is to spend every second of the day thinking about something else. Fighting like that makes you tired, and it doesn't matter how hard you fight anyway. They chip till they make a crack, and before you know it there's a ghost squatter in your living room. It's hard to get them out. Hard because they settle in. Hard because you like the company. If Grandpa's too tired to get a tree, then I'll go and bring one back for him. Someone in this family has to make contact with the Christmas spirit. "That's funny, Charlie," Mum says. I'm a funny kind of girl.

Dad's working in the shop. I walk in and tell him in a way that's meaningful, "Our family needs tinsel." He looks at me and says there's some in the third aisle. I go for the tree on my own.

It'd be a great plan if it included a map and a mobile phone. I left both at home. I'm about halfway to nowhere, taking a break under a tree and singing a punk version of "White Christmas" to distract myself from the heat of my nowhere-near-white Australian Christmas, when Mrs. Robbie's car pulls up.

Dave leans out of the passenger window. "What are you doing?"

It's a Christmas miracle. My words are back from vacation. "I'm just out enjoying the burning heat of the day." He grins, and I walk over to the car. "How'd you know it was me from the road?"

He doesn't answer my question, just flicks his eyes over Grandpa's old yellow rain boots, my short dress, and this hat that Gus says makes me look like the revolution's coming. I see his point. "You need a lift somewhere?" he asks.

"I'm going to the pine plantations for a tree."

"This road doesn't lead to the plantations. It doesn't really lead to anywhere."

I open the car door. "In that case, I'm going wherever it is you're going."

"Hi, love," Mrs. Robbie says. "Come to our place. You can have one of ours."

On the way to Dave's, we drive past the skeleton tree. There still aren't any leaves. But there's one bird sitting on a branch.

"So which one do you want?" Dave asks. The back section of the side paddock is covered in pine trees about the size of me. "Dad thought we could make some extra money at Christmas."

"I want that one." The tree I pick is breaking all the Christmas rules. It's lopsided, and one of its branches is longer than the rest. "It looks like it's giving us the finger."

"I'd be fairly pissed, too, if someone was about to hack me off, stick me in a living room, and throw me out come New Year's," Dave says.

"I'll decorate it."

"Then it should think itself lucky." He starts chopping. "Mum says she'll drive you back after lunch. You can ring home when we get to the house."

I watch the tree falling. "Dad and Grandpa won't notice I'm gone."

We carry it slowly up the hill, Dave leading the way. "So what's with the rain boots in summer? Is that some city thing?"

"Yeah, Dave. Plastic yellow rain boots are very in at the moment."

"Really?"

"Not really. I hate snakes."

"They're more scared of you than you are of them," he says.

"I don't think that's possible."

"In those boots, it's possible."

"Don't make me laugh. I'll drop the tree."

"This tree could only look better if you dropped it. You picked a shit tree," he says. It's not even that funny but we're laughing and I've got that crazy rubber hand thing happening so I can't grip the trunk. "Wait, wait. I need to stop."

We sit in the shade and catch our breath. "So, Rose says you're making her some music mixes." He leans back on his elbows. "Can you make one for me?"

"What sort of music do you like? Thrash, heavy metal, grunge?"

"Rose said you gave her some girls playing guitars. That sounds like something I'd like."

It feels like maybe we're talking in code, so I say, "I really love girls playing guitars." I lean back like he's leaning. Cool. Relaxed. But then I realize if we are talking in code, then I just told Dave I really love myself. He's not acting like I've said anything stupid, though. He's smiling.

"You ready?"

"I'm ready." I'm changing my name legally to Ready Duskin.

"What are you thinking?" Dave asks. "You've got a weird look on your face."

"But weird good, right?" I ask, picking up the tree.

"Right. Of course."

"I was thinking about changing my name. What would you change yours to?"

"I'm kind of comfortable with Dave."

"But if you needed a stage name, to give yourself some kick. Like Flea from the Red Hot Chili Peppers."

"He changed it to Flea?"

"I guess. I always figured his mum didn't name him Flea at birth." Bold move if she did. "I'd be Charlie Arabella Bird Duskin."

"Bird because you sing," he says. "Is your middle name really Arabella?"

"Yep. My mum's name is Arabella Charlie. I'm Charlie Arabella. She used to say I'm her turned inside out."

"I could be Dave Rolling Robbie."

"No you couldn't. That's a bad name. I can't let you have that name."

His dad walks out of the house. "You left the gate open. The cows could have been all over the road, you idiot."

Dave goes quiet. I put the tree down and stare at him. "Idiot doesn't really suit you, either," I say, and he's laughing as he walks into the house.

At Rose's place, dinner was this concert of laughter and noise and mess. Lunch at Dave's is quiet. Every time I clink my knife against the plate, it sounds as loud as if I've dropped it on the floor. "They didn't get out," Dave says when his dad goes on about the cows. He keeps going on, though, until Mrs. Robbie looks at him with concrete eyes and says, "They didn't get out."

Everyone eats quickly. His dad talks about work and the things that need to be done, about the snakes in the back paddock. It's not until he leaves that I realize I've been holding my breath.

"So, Charlie," Mrs. Robbie says while Dave clears the plates and puts on the kettle. "You look exactly like your mother. God, she was gorgeous." She pats my hand away from my face. "Stop that. Your smile's beautiful."

Mrs. Robbie waits in the car while Dave carries the tree into our living room. He spends ages putting it in a bucket, steadying it with bricks. "That should stay now."

"Thanks, Dave."

"So we're all going camping on the thirtieth. We'll be back on New Year's Eve." He waves and walks out the door.

I watch him go and try to remember the exact tune of his song. *So* we're all going camping. So *we're* all going camping. So we're *all* going camping. He could have meant a million things. He could have meant nothing at all. "Maybe he was asking you to go with them," Mum says.

"Maybe he needed a line to get out of the house," I say.

"Maybe if you worried less, you'd have more than two ghosts for friends," Gran says. Harsh, sure. But not entirely untrue. I start in with the tinsel.

Rose

I watch Dave heaving and dragging a Christmas tree into Charlie's house. Looks like he's finally working on something other than cars.

"Hi," I call as he walks out.

"Hi, Rosie. I told Charlie we were camping before New Year's."

I think about that for a second. "You told her we were going, or you invited her to come?"

"Shit," he says, and makes a sign to his mum that he'll be a minute. He goes back to her door, rehearsing what he's going to say. Charlie opens it before he knocks. Both of them look surprised. Dave laughs and walks inside. I sit on my front step waiting for the outcome. He walks out a while later, grinning.

"Happy Christmas," I tell him.

"Not Christmas till tomorrow, Rosie," he says.

Sure it isn't. Looks like New Year's won't be half so boring this year after all.

Charlie

I open the door to let in some breeze, and Dave's standing there. Both of us jump.

"Sorry. I was about to knock. Can I see the tree?"

"Sure. But it's only been five minutes. It pretty much looks the same except for one bit of tinsel." I walk down the corridor, and he follows.

"That piece of tinsel makes a big difference," he says.

"It's because it's expertly arranged. It's still a bit lopsided," I say, and lean my head over so the tree's not crooked.

"I like lopsided," he says, and keeps looking at it straight on. "So, before, when I said we were going camping, I meant you should come."

"Will there be snakes?"

"There are always snakes in the bush. You won't see them, though."

"That's comforting."

"Just make some noise to scare them off. You can wear those stylish boots, too," he says.

"Yeah. Okay. I'll come." I smile. I show him to the door. I close it.

And then I put on a Spiderbait CD and turn it up loud. "You're fucken awesome," I sing, and throw tinsel. "You're fucken awesome." Mum and Gran are dancing right here with me. We bounce down the hall. I'm about to go on the only date I've ever been asked on, and that calls for some kitchen moves. I'm yelling out lyrics and making toast when Dad walks in. "Good," he says. "You've got dinner."

At least I think that's what he says, because even though he walked through the living room, he didn't turn down the music. "I was thinking of this more as a predinner snack," I say.

"What?"

"I could go for some of your pasta," I yell.

He walks to the freezer and pulls out a container. "Not exactly what I had in mind, Dad."

"Sorry, Charlotte?"

"Hang on. I'll turn the music off."

He waves. "Don't worry. I'm going out. This doesn't wake Grandpa?"

"A truck speeding through his bedroom probably wouldn't wake Grandpa."

I don't know if Dad heard over the music. He checks that the buttons on his shirt are done up, which is the sign that he's not so happy with me. We don't say words like "truck" or "dead" or "cemetery." Apart from the funeral, we haven't been back there.

He leans in to kiss the top of my head but misses. "I'll see you tomorrow," he says.

"Of course you'll see me tomorrow. It's Christmas." He looks surprised. The lopsided tree flipping you the finger didn't give it away?

I turn off the music after he's gone and eat my microwaved gnocchi. One night when Mum was sick, I sat in Dad's office at the restaurant and watched him through the glass. Everyone was noisy except him. He chopped and fried and set out plates and helped people without yelling that they were too slow. In the middle of all that noise, no one noticed an apprentice's pan catch fire. The flames were huge but Dad leaned over and dropped a lid on it without saying a word. He saw me looking and winked. He's always been quiet but before Mum died it was a cool quiet that people really liked. He took notice of things. He took notice of me. I remember sitting next to him at the funeral. I didn't need him to say anything. I just needed him to look at me and wink.

The first summer here after Mum died, he visited old friends most nights. I fell asleep listening for his footsteps and I'd dream strange things like I was at the edge of the ocean, staring at opal water. I knew that Dad was underneath somewhere and the seaweed was holding him under. When I woke up, Gran was sitting by the bed.

"What about Dave's CD mix?" Mum asks, and she makes a good point. I leave a little plate of pasta for Grandpa in case a very loud truck detours in the night. I go into my room and choose some tunes. And the first one is by Spiderbait.

The only sound in the kitchen this morning is a humming fridge. I was hoping Dad would be humming in there while he cooked Christmas lunch but he must have come home late last night. The door to his room's closed. I sit outside. It's one of those mornings where the moon's still in the sky.

I hear opening cupboards after a while. Grandpa's out of bed before Dad, which is a first this summer. "You're cooking?" I ask, standing at the back door watching him.

"I had a dream your gran was yelling at me to get up and put the turkey in the oven."

"We're having turkey?"

He holds up a package from the freezer section of the shop. "With some imagination, it can be anything we want it to be."

Dad gets out of bed at eleven. He pours coffee and watches us cook. "Did you have a good time last night?" I ask, and he nods. "Who were you visiting?"

"Jen and Al Grace."

"I thought they moved to the city years ago," Grandpa says. "I'm sure they did."

"Is that turkey?" Dad asks.

"It says turkey on the pack." Grandpa looks over at him. "But I have serious doubts."

I set the table like Gran did, with bonbons and hats and streamers. We sit to eat, and everything looks like it should except for the empty chair next to Grandpa and the empty chair next to Dad. And except for Grandpa, who's still wearing his pajamas.

"Presents," I say after we finish. I got Grandpa some Johnny Cash, a little hardworking country music for a hardworking country man. I didn't know what to get Dad. In the end I went for a Nigella Lawson cookbook. I've seen him watching her shows every now and then, and I don't think it's entirely for the recipes.

His head stays straight on, so maybe he likes it. He hands his present to me, but I'm not too excited. Most Christmases he gets me a watch or a necklace I'd never wear. One Christmas he bought me a Britney Spears CD, which was so far off the mark I cried a little.

I pull off the paper and there's a Waifs CD, plus the single by Natalie Merchant and Gabriel Gordon. "Dad, thanks. I wanted these. Especially this." I hold up the single. "I've wanted this for ages."

"I have ears, Charlotte."

"But how did you find it?"

"Gus helped me."

I didn't even know he knew Gus's name. "I'll play it for you," I say. "There's this line of trumpet running through that hits you from the inside." He listens, and I watch to see if he hears what I do. There's something about the voice that makes me think of Mum.

"It's lovely, Charlotte," he says.

"You feel like you've heard it before, right?" I ask.

"Gus played it for me in the shop," he answers, which isn't what I want him to say. "That was a lovely dinner. If no one minds, I might take a walk. Catch up with some friends." That's definitely not what I want him to say.

He walks down the hall toward the front door, and I follow him. "Can I come with you? I'll be quiet. You won't know I'm there."

"It's not an easy day for your grandpa," he says. "Stay and keep him company." The tree flicks me the finger on my way through the living room. I flick one back. Solidarity. Christmas isn't always what you'd hoped for.

Grandpa and I eat cake in the garden after Dad leaves. "Can this be anything we imagine it to be, like the turkey?" I ask. "I'm imagining it's not stale. I'm imagining it's one like Dad used to make. Do you remember those?"

He nods. "I've been a bit behind on orders at the shop."

"It hasn't been long," I say. "You know, since Gran."

"Been long enough. The shop was her baby." He feeds his cake to the birds. "Why didn't you give your dad music for Christmas?"

"He doesn't listen to it."

"He did. I remember the first time he heard your mother play Gnossienne No. 1 at a school concert. She played the piano so beautifully."

"Erik Satie," I say. "They played it at the funeral."

"She loved that piece."

"I hate it." The notes sound like falling ice.

"Your father was only sixteen when he heard her playing it.

97

A country boy. I don't think he'd even heard classical music before then."

I hear Mum playing that song on the piano as Grandpa talks. I always asked her to stop; it made me think of ghosts even before she died. "Will all Christmases be like this one now that Gran's gone?" I ask.

"It'll get easier. We'll make new memories."

The birds and flies and clouds move slowly, like they hear Mum's ghost music, too. "What if we can't make new ones?" I ask.

"We have to, Charlie," he says. "If you can't do that, then you die."

Grandpa's asleep on the couch when Rose knocks this afternoon. I've been sitting near him, wishing he was awake and trying to get Mum's ghost music out of my head. "Come for a swim?" Rose asks. I get ready and grab the CD I burned and close the door, all in record time.

"I got something for you, too," she says after she opens my present. I unwrap a small, framed picture of the protistans. "Just one I got off the Internet. You can take it home."

"Thanks." I wrap it back in the paper so it won't break.

"Dave said you're making a CD for him, too."

"It might take a while." I wrote a big list last night, but I haven't made final decisions yet. The mix has to be exactly right. It has to say I'm cool enough to like retro, but I still know the latest music. It has to make him think he can't live without kissing me. That sort of CD could be years in the making.

"Christmas must be quiet without your gran," Rose says.

"A little. We ate something worse than what you cooked the other night."

"I thought your dad was a chef."

"He doesn't cook much at home anymore. But at the restaurant people line up around the block for his food. Before Mum died, she and I would go there every night and eat desserts he'd named after us. Charlotte Double Chocolate Cake. Arabella Lemon Mousse. Mum always said, 'Let's go halves in ourselves.'"

"You didn't eat there after she died?"

"Not much. I guess he was busy, and I got older."

"You're never too old for cake," she says. "Or mousse. Arabella's a cool name."

I like how Rose talks about Mum today, just throwing her out there. After the accident, the kids in my class avoided me. Like they thought they could catch my bad luck. Not Dahlia. She arrived the year after the accident, so she didn't know to be careful. "How come I never see your mum?" she asked one day.

"Because she died."

"I worry my mum will die," she said, and sat closer to me.

"Race you to the river." Rose runs and I chase, stumbling across rocks and grass and dirt. When we get there, she tosses her T-shirt and shorts onto the ground and dives into the water. "Hurry up, it's beautiful."

I'm wearing my bikini under my clothes, and I can still hear Louise calling me four-eyes. I'm not worried about what Rose thinks. I'm worried Dave'll appear out of nowhere. When he looks at me, I feel like I'm Clare Bowditch onstage with her band, singing these earthy songs about what I want and what I'm aching for. I'm sounding so sexy that my song's hitting him in the chest and stealing what he keeps there. Things might change if he sees me in my bikini.

I stand on the side, and Rose disappears, diving beneath the water, gliding and surfacing. "Come on," she yells, and it's hot, and so I think, Stuff it. Who cares what I look like? Louise, sure, but she's a long day's drive away. I peel off my shorts and throw myself into the water. "Shit. It's freezing."

"Bloody freezing," she says. "Keep moving."

I swim off Dad and Grandpa and the memory of Jeremy's party. I swim off that music they played at Mum's funeral. I swim till the ghosts in me are numb.

When we're drying off on the grass, Rose says, "I like your bathing suit. I've had this one for years. Luke likes it because it's almost see-through."

Somehow things don't matter today as much as they did. "I fell in the pool at the Year Ten party. My top came off in front of everyone."

She sits up and leans on one arm. "And?"

"And it's not a long story. The whole of Year Ten saw me naked."

"That's pretty bad. Still, I bet when you go back the guys'll be lining up to ask you out."

"I doubt it. I really humiliated myself."

"Yeah, but you really humiliated yourself naked. I hang out

with two guys. Trust me, the humiliation will fade and all they'll remember is the naked. Plus, you're pretty. Pretty girls get away with more."

"I'm not pretty."

"Dave thinks you are. He looks at you like you've got four wheels and a windscreen. He looks at you like you're a Porsche."

The sun drifts down but the air stays warm. Now that Rose says it, I did feel a little like a Porsche at the party. At least before I hit the pool. I think about Dahlia telling me that Alex was interested, about how happy she was because I was taking a risk.

She was so happy when I told her I'd changed my mind about auditioning for the school concert that she walked into a pole and we cracked up like old times. I crossed my fingers behind my back.

On the day of the tryouts I stood outside the door in case she checked. I listened to amazing voices flying past me and I was jealous. Not because they were singing better than me; I could sing like that. But I couldn't do it in front of all those people.

I walked away and when Dahlia asked how it went I gave her the thumbs-up sign. "But there were loads of people, so I probably won't get picked."

"What did you sing?" she asked.

"A Lemonheads track."

"And when do you find out?"

"They said a couple of weeks."

"What's the exact date you find out?" she asked, and I knew that she knew. "Louise was inside watching."

"She's such a bitch," I said.

"She might be a bitch sometimes, Charlie. But she doesn't lie."

"Are you okay?" Rose asks. "You're not sad?"

I don't want to tell Rose about Dahlia because it'll mix the sounds of that day with this one and I want them to start and end in different places. If Rose Butler likes me, I must finally be doing something right. "I'm okay," I tell her, and pull at the grass. "What about you? You don't ever get sad?"

She pulls her knees up to her chin. "Angry, sometimes. That's better than sad." Same coin, different sides, I think, remembering the funerals.

We stay till the moon appears. Huge and yellow. Sharing light with the sun. It makes me think of this song about a canary moon that Mum used to sing before I went to sleep. I'd mouth the words next to her. Tonight I almost feel like singing it aloud.

Rose

Charlie and I stay at the river till the light's gone. She's quiet at first like she always is but then she warms up a bit and tells me about being naked at a party, and she looks like she sees the funny side of things. I tell her she's pretty and that Dave thinks so, too, and her eyes fill right on up.

Mum acts as if Charlie's breakable. "Where are you going?" she asked before I left today. "Charlie's," I told her. "I'm taking a present."

"That's nice of you." She turned her teacup slowly in her hands. "What made you change your mind about her?"

I clicked my heels. "I guess I realized you were right."

"I wasn't born yesterday, Rose." She used her quiet voice, like saying I was lying in a whisper wasn't saying it at all.

"I'm sick of hanging out with guys all the time. Plus, Charlie's from the city. She's different to this place."

"Well, that makes sense," Mum said. "What are you giving her?"

"A picture of protistans. These things you can't see."

"She's had a hard time, Rose. You'll be nice to her?"

"She's not made of glass. I'm not swinging at her with a freaking bat." I picked at the best bits of turkey so I wouldn't have to meet her eyes.

I take a side look at Charlie. "Are you okay? You're not sad?"

"I'm okay," she says. Maybe her problem is that everyone's always telling her she's unhappy like Mum's always telling me I'm trouble. Maybe if we all lighten up, her eyes won't be so hard to look at. They might change to blue in the light.

"What about you? You don't ever get sad?" she asks.

"Angry, sometimes," I say. "That's better than sad."

We watch the moon for a while. It's almost red, a fiery sun somewhere giving out light so it can shine.

Canary Moon

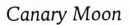

Sing, canary moon

Sing me sweet and yellow notes

Let them circle in the sky

Let them drift into my throat

I'll take them in

I'll swallow songs

I'll let them feather up my lungs

Let them feather up my blood

Sing, canary moon

Let me steal a little tune

And you won't even notice that it's gone

And when my belly's full

I'll canary into air

I'll canary with you, moon

And let all the people stare

I just won't care

I just won't care

I'll sing your yellow song

I'll sing it sweet

And loud and long

I'll sing it so it's heard

A million miles away from here

Sing, canary moon

Let me steal a little tune

And you won't even notice that it's gone

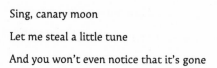

Charlie

Rose and I sit in the shade of her porch and eat ice. It's the twenty-seventh of December, and instead of counting the days till I go I'm wishing there were more days I could stay.

"You must miss Dahlia," Rose says.

"Yeah, but she rings me a lot. She e-mails, too. The first weekend I get back I'll sleep over at her place, talk about the summer. We might see a band that weekend."

"I wish I'd been born in the city. I should have been. Mum was in London when she found out she was pregnant."

"I don't know where Mum was when she found out about me," I say.

"You two look serious," Dave calls from a little way up the street. "Cheer up. Come for a ride." Rose points at two bikes

107

lounging on her lawn. She grabs hers and turns circles around me.

"It's been a while since I rode. You two go; I might help Dad in the shop." I haven't been on a bike since mine rusted in the shed. "Time to get back on," Mum says.

Rose gets off her bike and holds out a helmet. "Hop on." I search for balance and all the time I'm swaying Rose runs behind me, holding the back of the bike. I nearly drag her through the gravel, but she keeps up and runs till the rhythm becomes mine and I'm hypnotized by the shaky shapes I'm drawing. She lets go, and I glide. "You've got it!" she calls.

I'm not exactly sure what she thinks I've got as I jerk around the road, but whatever it is, I love it. I love the sound of the wheels purring like they did when I was a kid. "Miss me, miss me, miss me," they still say, but it's not sad. It's fast and full of blue sky whirring in the background.

All the sounds of the day mix together as I ride: Dave and Rose clapping, wind singing past my ears, laughter. My laughter. "There you go!" she yells as the wheels stop shaking. "That's it. Keep going. You've got it!"

Rose

"What exactly has she got?" Dave asks.

"I don't know, but I hope it's not catching."

He covers his eyes. "Is she doing a wheelie?"

"Not on purpose. She's funny, isn't she?"

"You just noticing that now?" he asks. I guess Dave's been watching her longer than me.

"Let's take her to the falls." The words are out of my mouth almost before I've thought them. The falls is the only place that's not quiet here. Dave and Luke don't know it, but sometimes I go there on my own. I go to scream. I go to tell the world to get lost under the run of the water. I stand till I'm drowning in something other than this place.

"Why, Rose?" Dave asks.

"I don't know," I say, and that's not a lie. "It feels like a place she should see." Charlie veers to the left in front of us, then straightens out at the last minute. "You make her ride to the falls, she'll kill herself," Dave says.

"Relax a little," I call.

"It's okay, Rose." She takes one hand off the handlebars to wave.

"Don't take your hands off the bars!" I yell too late. A rock kicks at the bike and sends her spinning across air with nothing to hold on to.

"Mayday, Mayday, she's going down," Dave laughs, and I close my eyes along with him. I can't look as she's forced into a tailspin and collides with the ground. "Maybe she should ride on my handlebars," he says.

"I think that's a very good idea."

"We should wait for Luke." He leans down to test the air pressure in his tires. "He finishes work in an hour."

"Not enough time if we want to get there and back before it rains." The three of us start out across the fields. Dave doesn't say a word as we ride into what we both know is a cloudless sky.

Charlie

"Hold your feet higher, Charlie," Dave says, pedaling up the hill.

"Maybe I could walk and meet you there?" My voice jumps with the bike over stones and dirt.

"It'd take too long. Just keep your feet off the ground." I turn to nod. "Shit, Charlie, no." He swerves sideways and hits a rock. The side of my arm slides across gravel and my front tooth sinks through skin.

"You two okay?" Rose calls back.

"I'm fine," I say, and haul my aching arse back onto the bars.

About halfway up the hill, Dave works out how to keep us steady. Instead of trying to ride in a straight line and hold the bike upright, he angles us toward the ground and swerves all over the road. "That's it," he says. "Perfect." Perfectly crooked. It's all in the way you look at things, I guess.

We make it to flat ground and he gets his breath back. "So, have you finished my CD?" he asks.

"Almost."

"How about you sing me one of the songs on it to pass the time?"

"I don't think so."

"You'd say no to a guy who's busting his arse to get you up a hill? That's cold, Charlie."

It is cold to say no to Dave. He does stuff all the time for people, like riding up hills and carrying Christmas trees. He even came to Gran's funeral with his mum and dad. I turned around before the service started and saw him sitting there. He didn't pull at his tie or scratch where his shirt itched him like some of the other guys. He was so still, staring at his hands. Afterward he stood beside his parents and nodded when they said sorry.

"I'm waiting," he tells me.

"You sing me a song."

"I'm pedaling," he says, but then he starts like a dog going crazy at the moon.

"Okay, stop. I'll sing."

"Too late. I've started."

"You sound like you're in pain."

"I'm pedaling up a hill with a girl on the handlebars while I'm singing. I am in fucking pain. No, don't laugh. Don't, you'll tip us. Don't. Shit."

We hit the ground again. "Bad things happen when you sing like that," I say.

"You're not wrong. I think I pulled a hamstring. Let's rest a bit before we climb to the falls."

"Climb?"

He points toward a figure on the edge of the hill waving to us.

"She's going up a cliff?"

For about five minutes, I try to walk upright and keep a safe distance between Dave and me. After the first fall, dignity goes out the window. I stumble over rocks and tree roots. Dave doesn't complain. He keeps catching me and saying it's not far. By the time we get to the top, we're covered in dirt.

Not for long. I stand under the waterfall while it smashes at rocks and skin and memory. Gus and Beth take me to bands when they can, when it's underage or they know the people running the gig. You walk inside, and the music's so loud the world shatters and the things that didn't make sense before still don't make sense but they don't have to while you're in there. That's what it's like here. The water makes everything ice and cracks it. I'm standing under bits of falling me. Dave and Rose are screaming, but I can't hear them. I scream back all the things I want in this world that I can't have. The water's making me cold and Dave's making me burn and I'm writing songs played with strings of sun and ice and honey.

"The best bit's not over," Dave says after we climb out. "Get on the bike and hold on. And don't think too much about it."

The three of us speed down the hill, Rose ahead and me on the bars of Dave's bike. I write a little tune on the way down that I call "The Screaming Song" because that's the only sound in it. "We're flying!" Dave yells as we move. "We are flying."

Rose

Charlie's screaming under the falls and Dave's yelling and I can't hear a word they're saying and it doesn't matter. All that matters here is letting go. Fuck boredom. Fuck being stuck in the middle of nowhere. Fuck being born with MADE IN THE BACK OF A HOLDEN stamped on your back. Fuck paddocks and plastic chairs.

I leave Charlie and Dave under the water and stand on the grass shaking my head, watching the last bits of the falls hit the air. I did an assignment on water at the end of this year. Luke and Dave were my partners, and I was doing most of the work, but Luke still complained the whole time. "Why do we have to do this? I already know about water. You drink it. End of story."

"Some people use it to wash occasionally, Luke," I said. "Which might be helpful for you to know." But then I tried to explain to him why I was so interested in it. "See, the water molecules are attracted to each other so much that they hold on for as long as they can. They grip at each other till they're too heavy and then they break. It's why water falls in tears." I wanted him to get it. I wanted him to see what it had to do with him and me. "Tell you what, Rosie," he said. "You finish the assignment and I'll go get us some fish and chips."

I ride down the hill in front of Charlie and Dave, the last of the water flying as I go. This bit's almost as good as the falls. It's the closest I can imagine to leaving.

We're dry by the time we hit town. We drop Charlie off and then Dave and I ride into my yard. Luke's waiting for us. "Where've you been?"

"We took Charlie to the falls. I think Dave likes her," I say, and Dave blushes.

"Right. She bent my handlebars."

"Isn't it about time a girl bent your handlebars?"

"Shut up, Rose."

"Maybe if you're nice to her, she'll let you bend her handlebars."

"Not interested."

"Liar. Here. She left her hat at my place." I throw it at him. "You should take it back to her."

"Why didn't you wait for me?" Luke kicks at the dirt. Dave doesn't tell him I said it would rain and I'm glad. The day's too bright for my lie. "We didn't think. I was so excited about taking her there. I didn't want to wait."

"I don't get why you two are all worked up about a chick from the city," he says, and storms off across the yard.

"What's wrong with him? He's been to the falls a million times."

"You ever been without him?" Dave asks.

I don't tell him I go all the time, without either of them. "It looked like rain."

"I have to go, Rose," he says. He's leaving to see if Luke's all right. They won't talk about me; they'll play video games until Luke laughs again.

The first spits of summer rain land on my face but stop as soon as they begin. "See, I didn't lie," I call out, but it's too late. I'm already alone.

Sometimes I wonder why I love Luke so much when he makes me this mad. But then I remember how I felt when he kissed me in Year 6. He didn't do it again until Year 8, and he only did it then because I told him to.

I'd been waiting and waiting for him to ask me to the social. "Well? Are we going together?"

"What? I don't know. Yeah. We go everywhere together." I was so pissed off. "Unless you ask me, I'm going with Michael Howsware."

"So go with him."

"I will." Idiot. Stupid idiot. "I'll let him kiss me, too."

Luke snarled. "Do whatever you like."

"Rose, you look beautiful," Mum said before I left that night; I didn't care, though. What did it matter if I had to go with Michael? We walked in and Luke was dancing as close as the teachers would let him with Andrea Cushifsky. *Andrea Cushifsky.*

I danced next to Luke and grabbed Michael tight. I held on even though I was gagging on cheap aftershave. I tried so hard to remember how I'd felt when Luke kissed me and to feel it for Michael; but he wasn't the one who sat with me all Sunday at the edge of the freeway. He wasn't the one who bought me tiny cars for Christmas. "Just a car," Luke said. "You don't have to get so excited." But I was excited because he'd noticed what no one else had.

Luke and Andrea disappeared about eight-thirty. Most kids made a stop at the back of the sports equipment shed sometime during the night, but I couldn't believe Luke would take Andrea there.

I waited till Michael went to the toilet, then I slipped outside. I leaned forward as far as I could without being seen. And there they were. Sitting at opposite ends of the fence, staring separate stares across the oval.

Luke was such an idiot. If I hadn't come round the corner, he would have pretended he'd kissed Andrea, and loved it. I watched till she got sick of waiting and went back inside. Then I walked round the corner in my fantastic dress and sat on the end of the fence.

"What are you doing here?"

"Waiting for Michael." I smiled. "He'll be out in a minute."

Luke looked so hurt that I let him get away with stuffing up my first dance. "You idiot," I said. And I moved close to him on the fence, swinging my legs while the wood caught at my stockings, making holes in them. The leaves blew off the trees and scattered color. In the light from the gym they looked like tiny pink tongues.

* * *

I climb into the old tree. Its branches are thick enough to sit on, but I've never done it before. I can see the whole of Charlie's yard from here. I never knew the garden next door was so green, so overgrown. She's sitting outside holding her guitar and smiling. I've never seen her relaxed like that.

"Rose?" Luke calls from the back door. "You out here? I'm sorry I got mad." I curl my legs up in the leaves and hold my breath. Part of me wants to go down and talk to him, and the other part of me holds tighter to the tree. "She's not out there, Mrs. Butler!" Luke shouts, and I stay till I hear the front door close.

"Rose?" Mum calls from the living room as I come inside. "Luke was looking for you. He said you weren't in the yard."

"Didn't hear him. I must have been dreaming."

She stares at me for a second. "Be careful, Rosie. People hurt easy."

"You don't have to worry about Luke."

"It's not him I'm worried about," she says.

Mum and I have heaps of almost conversations these days. She almost asks me what's wrong and I almost tell her. What would I say if I did? That I can't decide what's worse, the dreams I have where I can't find her or Dad or the dreams I have where I'm crying because I can't get away?

"You don't need to worry about me, Mum. I'm fine," I say. And we both keep pretending that I am.

Charlie

Dave rides me to my door after the falls. He and Rose leave and I sit in the garden, singing my song about the day. About an hour later he comes back. "You left this at Rose's," he says, holding out my hat.

He stands there, rolling his bike back and forward, and I want to ask him in. For a girl who doesn't talk all that much, strangely I have a million or more things I want to say to Dave. They're not even important things. It's stuff like Grandpa ordered in some *Muppet Show* toothbrushes, and I've been using one even though it's too small because I really like Fozzie Bear. But then I stopped using it because I wasn't sure if it was a sign of respect to use Fozzie that way.

That's the stuff I want to tell him but I've been talking to him all day and Louise says guys don't like it when you act keen. I'm not acting keen, I think, looking at Dave. I am keen. But Louise says if you're not absolutely gorgeous, you should play hard to get. "Play hard to get, Charlie," she said once. "Act cool. Sometimes you look a little desperate."

So I don't tell Dave about my Fozzie Bear toothbrush dilemma. I thank him for my hat and close the door. Sure, I want to open it straight back up and yell his name but I don't. I draw a line between me and uncool and I don't cross it.

Instead I put on a Fiona Apple CD and turn her up loud. I told Gus once about Louise and how she treated me and he said, "Some people are hard to understand, so you gotta understand yourself." He played some Fiona. "It's what Beth listens to on days when she says I am not the biz." That music folded Louise in two and put her in a drawer.

I dance to my loud music. Oh yeah, I'm sassy. I'm hard to get, that's what I am. Hard. To. Get. Cool. I slide to the fridge and grab a Coke. I slide back. "What are you up to?" Grandpa asks, walking into the kitchen.

"I'm being sassy. Playing hard to get. Cool. Not desperate."

"Dave Robbie's riding his bike around our front yard. Any idea why?"

In case of fire, it's good to know we can all get out of the house in less than five seconds. I take a breath and open the door. "Hi. Did you forget something?"

He shakes his head. "I just didn't want to go home."

Fuck cool. Cool is overrated. "You want to stay for dinner?" He throws his bike down and follows me inside.

"Hi, Mr. Duskin," he says to Grandpa. "What's up?"

"Well, you just missed Charlie doing her sassy dance."

"He's old," I say, pulling out pasta. "Losing his mind."

"I wasn't the one sassy dancing. What's news with you, Dave?"

"We went to the falls this afternoon."

"All the way up there? Tell your dad that, Charlie. He and your mother lived at that place when they were teenagers. 'Up to no good,' your gran used to say."

Dad's not back by the time we eat, so it's just the three of us sitting in Gran's garden. "How's the shop going, Mr. Duskin?" Dave asks. And the two of them talk about cars and drought and Gran and footy. Dave's got being cool without being cool down to an art.

After dinner Grandpa shuffles off to watch TV. Dave helps me clean up. His tattoo of a bird flaps its wings against the crease of his wrist. Gliding and dipping while he washes the dishes. The inside of me glides and dips with it. I think about a song I might write, one where I'm washing dishes next to Dave and his tattoo. Parts would be fast, like I'm feeling inside, but parts would be slow and quiet like Dave is tonight, taking time to talk to Grandpa. It would have wings, feathers tickling under my skin, flying all the way to my throat.

Dave washes the last pot, and I worry about what we'll do after we finish. I've only really liked a few guys before. There was Ayden Smith, who I told to piss off. Alex Martin, which ended, you know, at the bottom of a pool. And Leo Gordon, one of the popular guys that Louise hangs out with.

Maybe Dahlia asked Louise to set me up with Leo. I'm not sure. We didn't even really have a date. We all went out as a group and I said about three words to him, all to do with music. He told me he liked the Clash, so I burned him a few tracks. That's when Louise suggested I act a little less desperate. It was the fucking Clash, I wanted to yell. It's not like I gave him Celine Dion.

Dave dries his hands. "It's quiet. Where's your dad?"

"I don't know. He usually visits friends at night."

"And what do you do?"

"Listen to music, mostly."

"So put some on."

"The stereo's in the living room. Grandpa's watching TV. My laptop's in my bedroom." I mean I'll go and get it, but Dave follows me. He walks around and looks at my stuff. "Who's that?" he asks, staring at the picture above my bed.

"The bassist from the Clash. Paul Simonon."

"He's smashing his guitar," Dave says.

"Jimi Hendrix burned his guitar. A Fender Stratocaster."

"A what?"

"A very cool guitar."

"Then why'd he burn it?"

"He said you sacrifice the things you love."

Dave thinks for a bit. "I love my car. I bought an old Hummer I'm doing up in my spare time. No way I'd set fire to it. Would you burn all your CDs?"

"If it meant getting something I wanted more. But that's a different thing, I guess."

"You go out to bands, dance?" he asks.

"I'm a pretty shit dancer."

"So am I. They have these school socials, and I go because Luke and Rose do, but I stand there on the side feeling like an idiot."

"You could always do the half dance," I say. "You know, sit and move your hands around." I choose a song with a kicker beat and give him a little demo. He sits next to me on the bed. "How am I doing?" he asks.

"Almost as good as you are at singing."

"Lucky I don't know the words, hey?" He slides into some strangely impressive moves. I don't tell him about the Fozzie toothbrush in the end. Turns out sitting next to him half dancing is even better than talking. We're listening to the Stones when Dad puts his head in. I'm sitting on the bed with a guy who's wearing a black singlet and faded jeans and has a tattoo on his wrist listening to a song about wanting some satisfaction and all Dad says is "Just letting you know I'm home" before he closes the door.

"I better go," Dave says.

I walk him out, and he gets on his bike. He rides around me a couple of times, half dancing, then grins and takes off up the street.

I walk back inside, half dancing a little myself, and stand outside Dad's door. I turn off the lights in the hallway and get down on my hands and knees to check if his light's still on. I want to tell him I went to the falls and see what he says.

"Drop something, Charlie?" Grandpa asks from behind me.

"A while ago," I say, standing up. "It doesn't matter." I kiss him good night. I lie on my bed, staring at the poster of Paul Simonon, wondering how it would feel to be a person who could smash things.

After a while Mum tells me that she and Dad did go to the falls. She tells me it was exciting, like it was for me and Dave. I think about him dancing on the bed, and Mum says, "It was definitely a sugar day, Charlie." That's what she always said when things went well for me.

"It was the best sugar day ever," I tell her, and I sing about it. I sing the kind of song that used to make Dahlia and me laugh. A song in major chords.

Sugar Days

Lazy days

And sweet sun shining

Holding hands would be so fine

And kissing you would be so finer

Would turn my skin and blood to sugar

Would turn my mouth to sunny butter

Voice to milk

Brain to flour

Sifted through your hands

I'm cake

Please kiss me into sugar days

Kiss me till I'm chocolate

Till I'm hot chocolate

Till I'm frosted Froot Loops that you can't stop
    eating from the box even when it's not break-
    fast time anymore

Till I'm double-chocolate-chip ice cream

The one that hints at peppermint but you're never
    really sure

Please kiss me more

Kiss me till I'm a Mars bar
Kiss me till I'm a freaking box of Mars bars
On top of another box of Mars bars
Kiss me till I am on a sugar high
And flying

Rose

I've been to our camping spot a hundred times but it's always the same—you never find it without getting lost first. When we were kids, Dad made us tie ribbons on the trees that led in from the road. "If you can't find the way back to the site, follow the markers," he said. I guess he figured sooner or later Luke would do something stupid and convince us to go wandering at night.

"Got your ribbons?" he asked before I left today. I patted my bag. I put them in more for Charlie than me. She doesn't know the bush.

She catches her breath when we come round the corner. In the middle of the dryness you forget that places like this exist. The river opens all of a sudden; it's wider here than anywhere else, and on a still night you get the feeling if you jumped through it'd shatter.

"It's gorgeous," Charlie says. "I've never been camping before."

"You're here every summer," Dave says. "I would've thought you'd been loads."

"Dad's never around long enough, and there's the shop to run."

"And if her grandpa took her camping, there'd be no hamburgers and chips," Luke says.

"Is that all you think about?" Dave asks. "Burgers and chips?"

"Mostly I think about sex."

"You're a dickhead." Dave looks embarrassed, which I'm thinking is because Luke said "sex" in front of Charlie. Luke can say "sex" as much as he likes, but he's not getting that from me. Not in the back of a car. Not in a tent. Not in a million years.

I'm here to look at this place one last time before I ask Charlie to help me get to the city and things change for good. I'm visiting so I can remember it when I'm gone.

"Why's it so cold tonight?" Luke asks. But we get nights like this in summer every now and then; the wind starts up and the sky cracks when you're expecting it to stay still.

Dave stares at Charlie and keeps shifting closer to her, and every time he does she sits even stiller, like that river. I get the feeling it's a different story on the inside of her. She says she has to go to the toilet, and Dave's up before she is, showing her the way.

"So Dave's on with the Dorkin," Luke says after they've gone.

"Luke, don't hassle them."

"Did I miss something? Are you and Charlie best friends now?"

"I like her."

"You used to call her Charlie Dorkin all the time, remember?" He hunches his shoulders and brushes his hair into his face.

I try not to laugh. "Stop it."

"She can't think for herself. She follows everything you do."

"Shhh . . ." I reach over and put my hand on his mouth. I don't want him to be angry tonight. This could be the last camping trip we have.

Dave comes back before Charlie. "She said she could find her own way."

Luke pushes my hand off his mouth. "Do you remember Rose making up that song about Charlie?"

"I never sang it to her face."

"You sang it in your backyard once." Dave looks over his shoulder.

"Charlie Dorkin, Charlie Dorkin . . . ," Luke sings.

"Do you think she heard me?" I ask, laughing because Luke's making this stupid face at me.

"Probably," Dave says. "What does it matter now?"

Luke sings it again.

"Shut up. She'll be back soon." Dave swings the torch over us. The light casts shadow monsters on our skin.

Charlie

Dave stands and stretches and then sits back closer to me. He's done that about five times and I work out there's only one stretch till there's no air between us. I've got stars in my blood, burning light under my skin.

"I have to use the bathroom," I say, and he stands before I've finished my sentence. We walk close; there's almost nothing between us. Our torches throw light ahead but we're in shadows behind them. Dave's the smell of oil and grass and the sound of cracking sticks. I'm stumbling breath.

There's one small light on over the toilet block. He shuffles underneath it. "Can you find your way back?" he asks.

"I'll follow the markers Rose left. Snakes sleep at night, yeah?"

"Of course," he says, and I don't know if he's telling the truth or lying to make me feel better.

I'm quick because of the possible snakes and because I think that when I get back I might sit that last stretch closer. I might actually get some of the things I'm wanting. A summer of Dave, of swimming at the river, of going to the falls, of kissing.

I stop for a minute in the trees at the edge of our camp so I can take in the sounds and write about them later. Cicadas and mosquitoes. Night birds. Water not far away. Luke and Rose and Dave laughing.

The name Dorkin stops me like a bullet. It sinks past my clothes and into my chest. It's Luke who sings it, but I don't care about him. I care about Rose laughing. "She'll be back soon," Dave says, and that hurts more than Luke and Rose put together. She. He didn't even use my name.

I stand in the cold, the twigs scratching at my legs. I stand there going over the day at the falls and how he danced with me and how he talked to my grandpa, and none of it makes sense. Why would a guy do all of that and then laugh behind my back? Unless it was a joke. I imagine what Louise would say. I mean, why else would a guy not make a move when he's in your bedroom, Charlie? Hello. Wake up.

I'm awake. I'm wide awake. Who does something like this to someone? "Charlie, are you lost?" Dave calls through the trees. "Follow the markers Rose left." I don't move. Those markers don't lead anywhere I want to go.

When I'm playing the guitar, my hands move by instinct.

I don't think about chord changes or whether I can make them fast enough. I just do it. My instinct's telling me to walk out of here tonight. It's telling me to stop at the camp for a second. Long enough to say, You're all dickheads. Long enough to look Rose Butler in the eyes and tell her she's a bitch.

But it's dark and I won't find my way to the road on my own. So I stay where I am until Dave's footsteps come toward me. I let him lead me back to the others. "I didn't notice I was lost till it was too late," I say.

For the rest of the night, Dave passes me marshmallows. There's no fire but they're ash in my mouth. Every time they laugh, I hear my name: Charlie Dorkin. Rose's eyes are hidden by shadow, but I imagine they're mean now, like thick lemon skin, bright as the sun but sour underneath.

"Night, Charlie," Rose says. Luke makes a sign with his hands and my face burns. I watch as they disappear into one tent. No one talked about where we'd sleep. I thought Rose and I would share. So this is why they asked me. The last part of the plan is for Dave to make me feel like a complete idiot. There are idiots here, but I'm not one of them.

I wrap my jumper tight around me and move away from him. We sit like that for a long time, not saying anything. He looks confused but I don't explain. Work it out for yourself, wanker.

"I'm going to sleep," Dave says eventually. "Here." He throws his jacket beside me. "If you're sitting up, you'll need this."

I stare at my hands until I hear the tent flap zip. I wait until the cold sinks into me and settles for the night. I wait until I think Dave will be asleep and then I slip into the sleeping bag next to him. I concentrate on being still as the sides of the tent breathe in and out around us.

"Is something wrong?" Dave's voice runs down my arms and fingers. His breath smells of marshmallows and chips and oil and grass and waiting. Waiting for someone who's mine. This isn't real, though. Dave doesn't like me. There's no point in thinking about his breath. That breath is not for me. His bird tattoo is not for me, either, or his jokes or his half-dancing ways.

"I didn't know about the tents," he says. "I didn't plan anything."

It finally starts to rain, soft trails of water running down the canvas. "'Storm' is a funny word," he says, but I pretend to be asleep. I really wish I had my guitar. I don't want to sing to Dave. I want to smash him over the head with it.

A Slightly Longer Wanting Song

It's just a slightly longer wanting song

It still won't take me all that long

Just long enough to say

How much I'm wishing for

Just a little more

Than what I wished that song before

Rose

Charlie comes back from the bathroom restless, eating marsh-mallows that Dave passes her, looking at her watch and out into the bush. She's waiting for something and I know how she feels. Luke shines the torch in my face and I close my eyes and see city lights. I open them and she's staring. I smile.

"What's up with you?" Luke asks. I kiss him and laugh. I'm not staring at cars tonight. The road's in me. Tomorrow Charlie'll tell me what happened with Dave, and I'll tell her about the scholarship, and she'll invite me to stay with her. The interview's at the end of January. If Charlie asks her dad after New Year's Eve, and Mum and Dad agree, I can be gone by next month. I kiss Luke again. "Night," I say. Luke gives Dave a not-so-secret sign and I punch him. It's not me who's always pushing. Inside the tent we kiss like I knew we would. I want this and I want to be away at the same time. His hands move farther and my skin sparks and I keep thinking that if I don't leave this town soon I'll do this with Luke. I'll do it and be like Mum. Stuck in a town because of one stupid mistake. I push his hands off.

"What?"

"Nothing. I'm tired."

I know Luke. Know how he breathes when he's confused. Know how he breathes before he falls into sleep. I lie next to him and listen to him snoring. Nothing'll wake him now.

"Luke," I whisper, so quiet I can barely hear myself. I sort of mouth it; it's not like I'm cheating, saying it while he's sleeping. I'm practicing; I can't tell him when he's awake yet, and it's squashing against my chest more with every day that I don't say it.

"There's something I have to tell you. Don't be angry, but I'm leaving at the end of summer. See, I passed this test and won a scholarship. Mrs. Wesson told me about it. I get to do Years Eleven and Twelve at this great school. And that's why I don't want to, you know, do anything with you that might make me have to stay. Like Mum did with Dad. She'd be halfway across the world right now if she hadn't . . . I've been thinking about that a lot. How one mistake changed her whole life and—"

"Rosie?" His voice cuts me off and I freeze. "I'm not asleep."

Shit.

He leans up on his elbow and blinks a bit so his eyes adjust to the darkness. "When did you find out?"

137

"Before the holidays. I was going to tell you."

"So how come you didn't?"

"I don't know. I wasn't sure what you'd think."

"I bet you told your new friend," he says.

"I didn't. Mum might not even let me go. Luke, don't say anything yet."

He's quiet for a minute and the rain starts to fall. "That's it. You want to leave with her. You're using her."

"I'm not. I like Charlie."

"Bullshit. She's your ticket out of this place."

"Please don't tell her yet."

He turns over without answering. I feel like Luke and I are on an island that's sinking and there's nothing I can do to stop it. I can swim, though. If Luke can't, then it's too bad. He's had sixteen years to learn.

Everyone's quiet on the way out. It's late afternoon and I don't think we've said more than five words all day. Dave stays behind me. Luke strides out in front. Charlie walks to the side of all of us, snapping off branches as she moves.

"What did you do to her, Dave?" I ask after she goes inside her house.

"I didn't do a thing. She wouldn't even talk to me."

"Well, somebody did something. Luke?"

"What about you, Rose?" Dave snaps. "That was stupid, making her share a tent with me. Did you think that was funny?"

"No. I thought—"

"I don't reckon you thought at all."

The three of us stare at each other. Dave never yells. And he never yells at me. "Just forget it," he says, and walks away.

"I guess since you're leaving, you don't need us anymore. Don't you care about Dave, either?"

"You can talk. You're the one who gets him in trouble with his dad all the time."

"What's that got to do with you? Dave can do what he likes." He spits on the ground.

"That's disgusting, Luke."

"No, Rose," he says. "That's not what's disgusting."

Charlie

The problem with the world isn't that there are too many liars. The problem is that people aren't good enough at it. Who said nobody likes a liar? I like liars. I love liars. "Charlie, you are beautiful. Everybody loves you, Charlie Duskin." I could do with a bit of that.

I'm working on a couple of new songs. I can't decide between "Dave Robbie Is a Total Loser/Moron/Wanker," "Dave Robbie Picks His Nose and Eats It," "Where the Fuck Is Dad?" or, my personal favorite, "Shove This Song Up Your Arse, Rose Butler." I play them loud. I play them till the walls throw them back at me. No one comes and asks what's wrong. I play louder. Still no one. "Is Everyone in This Place Deaf?" I thrash out loudly. Apparently, yes.

I take my guitar on tour instead. We walk around the house. Grandpa's left a note to wake him when dinner's ready. Dad's left a note to say he's in the shop and not to worry about food for him. If he's in the shop, surely he hears me and my angry guitar song. What would my note say? "Notice me, notice me, notice me." I play some chords loudly to go with it. What sort of dad needs a note to work that out about his daughter? Gus and Beth notice things about me and they lived through the sixties.

Dahlia used to say I had a dad other kids dreamed about. "He never yells, he wouldn't notice if you sneaked out, and he cooks the best chocolate cake I've ever tasted. What more do you want?"

I want a whole lot more. I want someone to talk to. I want someone who can fix things when they're broken. I want to scream and have someone come running down the hall in their slippers, out of breath with worry.

I strike up another verse of "Dave Robbie Is a Total Wanker." I play it as loud as I can outside Grandpa's room. The world has lost its ears today. I'm screaming and no one can hear me.

"Charlie?" Rose calls, and knocks on the back door. I don't answer. What's the point, when everything she says is a lie? She's still shouting when I walk through to the shop. I'm changing my name to Risk-taker. Dave can keep Rolling Idiot Robbie. It suits him. I storm into Dad like a runaway guitar riff, ripping at the air. Don't think I have a plan, though. I never do.

Rose

I knock for ages on Charlie's door. Eventually I give up and ride out to Dave's. I sit next to him at the kitchen table and feel weird because neither of us says anything about what happened on the camping trip.

I know he's forgiven me when he takes out this book on Formula One racing and starts showing me the pictures. "Look at this guy, Rosie. He's on fire."

"Right, fire. He's going fast then, huh?" I wish Dave would talk to me about what he thinks is wrong with Charlie, but he keeps going on about the cars.

"Are you even listening? I mean he's actually *on fire*." Dave shoves the book in my face again.

"I can't see any flames."

"It's an ethereal fire."

"You mean ethanol, Dave. It makes a clear flame."

"Whatever. He was burning in front of everyone and they didn't even know." Dave goes on and on in the background, but I can't concentrate. I keep seeing Charlie's face on the way home today. White ash. If Dave and Luke didn't upset her, then that only leaves me.

"They walked up to find out what was wrong with him and they caught fire, too," Dave says.

"Shit."

"I know. He was dead before anyone worked out what was going on."

"No, I mean, shit, I have to find Charlie."

"Why, you know what's wrong with her?"

"She heard us last night, Dave. When we called her Charlie Dorkin." That has to be it. And she's been burning ever since. Except no one was taking enough notice of her to see.

Charlie

Dad's counting the till when I storm in. It takes me about a second to lose my steam. "Charlotte, you're back." Looking on the bright side, I guess he noticed I was gone. "How was the camping trip?"

I want to tell him how awful it was, how I heard them all making fun of me. You raised a Dorkin. But then I'd have to explain to him what a Dorkin was and I'd feel worse after I finished than when I started. So instead I say, "There are animals in the bush, Dad. Dangerous animals."

"Lucky you came back in one piece, then, Charlotte," he says in his funny voice.

Look a little closer, Dad, I think, and ring the bell. "I'll be outside having a Coke."

After a while, one of the kids from the town sits beside me. I've seen him around but he hardly ever comes into the shop. "You don't look so good," he says. "I'm Antony Barellan, a friend of Rose and Luke's."

"I'm Charlie."

"I know. That's your dad in there, isn't it?" He nods toward the shop.

"Uh-huh."

"It was crappy that your gran died. My parents knew her. They said she was really nice."

"She was nice," I say, looking at the scratches on my hands from the camping trip. "Really nice."

"So you're only here for the summer, right?" He kicks at the chair and stares across the street. "You're lucky. What do you do for fun in the city?"

I sit on my own and play guitar to ghosts, I think as Rose walks up. She scowls at Antony. "What are you guys up to?"

"I was just telling Charlie how boring it is around here."

"Then maybe you should leave, Antony."

He rubs his middle finger down his nose. "Luke," he calls past her.

Luke arrives and ignores Rose. He sits in the middle of Antony and me and puts his arms around the two of us. "What's going on?"

"Nothing. Haven't even got money for cigarettes." Antony grins in my direction. "Think you could get some from your dad, Charlie?"

"No, she can't," Rose says.

"I didn't ask you, did I?"

She turns her back to him. "Come on, Charlie." She moves without checking to see if I'm getting up, like a dog she's owned for years. "I can get cigarettes," I say. Shove that song up your arse, Rose Butler. Not everyone does what you tell them to do.

"Well, all right." Antony grins.

"I'll meet you by the river after I get them." And it'd be good if you could have an ambulance waiting because I think I'm about to have a heart attack. They're right. Smoking does kill.

Gran always said the shop would be mine when she and Grandpa died. Technically this isn't stealing. It's gift giving and this is the holiday season so I shouldn't feel guilty. I should feel like Santa. "Santa doesn't steal," Mum says. It's times like these I could really do without a dead mum looking over my shoulder.

Dad's standing behind the cash register, right in front of the cigarettes. I need a diversion, that's all. A simple, nothing-can-go-wrong diversion. The problem with kids like me is I've got no imagination for bad. The baddest thing I've done is stick gum under the table in class, not exactly a call-the-police offense. I back out of the shop planning to abandon my life of almost crime but Antony's waiting there. His hand covers my mouth.

"Charlie . . ." His breath is warm and wrapped in chips. "Thought you'd need a bit of help." He's pressed so hard against my back my insides are sprinting. Now I'm sure I need

146

that ambulance. "Listen. You go and distract him, and I'll take the stuff." He pushes me forward.

I walk inside. "Charlotte?" Dad says. "Charlotte, what's the matter?" He steps out from behind the counter and moves toward me. I walk through to the kitchen and that's when I break a lifetime habit and really cry in front of him. I start and I can't stop. I want him to fix this mess, for him to hear Antony in the shop and kick him out. But he just stands there with his hands hanging and his head tilting to the side.

"It'll be all right," he keeps saying, and I want to shout, Get some new freaking glasses, Dad. I'm stealing from you. There's no way it's going to be all right.

I rain out tears. Over Dad's shoulder I see Antony sneaking behind the counter pouring packets of cigarettes into his bag. If Dad turns the smallest bit, he'll see him, too, but he doesn't. He stares at his hands like he's forgotten what they're for. Antony does his best to hide the gap on the shelf while I wish with every part of my body that I could hide in Dad's arms. I watch Antony give me the thumbs-up in the background and I stand there and cry even harder.

Rose

It takes all my self-control not to kill Luke while we wait for Charlie and Antony at the river. He's wearing this stupid look on his face like all his Christmases have come at once. I want to grab him by the neck and say, You dickhead, there's more at stake here than you. I'm not thinking about the scholarship, either. I've broken Charlie.

I can tell she's been crying when they get back. "Are you okay?" I ask, but she ignores me.

"So, what's next?" Luke lights up a cigarette.

"It's New Year's Eve," Antony says. "We need alcohol."

There are only two places they'll be able to get any. Either Luke will steal it from his parents or they'll go to Arthur's bottle shop on the edge of town. A lot of kids have tried to steal from there and they've all ended up in jail. They've been happy for the bars after Arthur threatens them with these dogs he keeps hungry on nights like New Year's Eve.

It's the sort of thing Luke talks about when he's trying to sound tough. "I could steal from Arthur," he'd brag, and I'd laugh.

"In your dreams, buddy," Dave would say. But we're not in Luke's dreams today. We're in my nightmare. I don't care about Antony, but if I know one thing for sure—he won't take the stuff himself. He'll find some way of convincing Luke and Charlie to do it.

"Luke, don't," I say. "You'll get caught."

"You can't tell me what to do," he says, and the three of them stand up. I catch Charlie's arm. "I know why you're mad. I'm sorry." She barely looks at me before walking away.

"Happy New Year, Rose," Antony says.

"Don't get too happy yet, Antony," I tell him.

And then I run as fast as I can to get Dave. Branches scratch at my legs and leave thin streaks of red, but I keep moving.

I bang on the door till he opens it. "You have to come with me."

"I can't. Dad's not happy I forgot to mow the back paddock before I went camping. I said I'd have it done by the time he and Mum get back."

"It's Luke and Charlie." He still doesn't move. "And Antony Barellan."

"What are they doing?" Dave asks. I can tell he's still not

sure if it's worth annoying his dad for. I want to protect Charlie a little if I can, but it's too late for that now. "She stole some cigarettes."

"My dad'll kill me tonight if I don't mow the paddock and she's got a while before lung cancer kicks in so I think I'll let her cool down a bit." He walks toward the shed.

"Antony was talking about taking alcohol from Arthur's."

"Okay, that's different," he says, and we run for the gate.

There's no sign of them at the bottle shop. They're not at the river, either. "Where do you think they are?" I ask.

"They've maybe got some alcohol, and it's a nice night. Antony'll be looking for a place to drink it."

"The quarry?" I ask.

"They couldn't get there without a car," Dave says. "You think they're dumb enough to steal one?" Neither of us bothers answering. We're talking about Luke Holly and Antony Barellan.

"I guess I'll ride out and check," Dave says. "You go home."

"No way. I want to be the first to kill Luke."

"I'll kill Antony and bring Luke back alive. You can kill him then. But you need to ring Charlie's grandpa and tell him she's staying with you so she doesn't get in trouble. You need to be home to cover for her if he checks."

"Find her, Dave." Charlie's been through a lot. She shouldn't have to add spending New Year's Eve with Antony Barellan to the list.

Charlie

Shit. I'm in trouble. When I wished for people to take notice of me, I was thinking concert, not court of law. At least Luke didn't go through with stealing from the bottle shop. He looked at the dogs and decided it would be better to steal from his parents.

"Where are we going now?" I ask.

"The old quarry," Antony says. "We won't get caught there."

"It's miles away. We'll be walking all night."

"But we're not walking, Charlie." He pulls a clip out of my hair and uses it to pick the lock of the car we're standing in front of. Shit. I'm not entirely unconnected to the crime scene.

"Get in," Antony says.

"I don't want to get in. I want to go home."

A porch light shines and we're in clear view. "Get the fuck in." Antony pushes me. "You want to get caught?"

Luke gets in, too, and Antony hot-wires the car. "Remember your seat belts." He laughs and takes the car from zero to a hundred in a minute. He takes huge swigs from his beer at the same time.

"Charlie, relax." Antony stares at me in the rearview mirror. "You look like you're scared half to death." That's only because I like my drunk driver to have his eyes on the road and both hands on the wheel. "This is no time for jokes, Charlie," Mum says.

"I know, I know, I know," I say, and Antony asks me what I know and I think: I know you're a dickhead. "Nothing," I say. "I know nothing."

I start playing "Where the Fuck Is Dad?" in my head. I've heard stories about fathers who can sense that their daughters are in trouble. "Where the fuck is Dad? Dad. Dad. Dad." My fingers tap the panicked rhythm on the car door. After a while I change my song to "Who the Fuck Am I Kidding?" My dad couldn't sense me if I was screaming in his face. The only person left to save me now is me. That really makes me wish I had a plan.

The car swoops from one side of the road to the other like a bird dazed by light. My stomach is swooping, too. It's dark and I can't see much of anything outside the window. Even if I could get Antony to stop the car, I'd be lost.

He brakes on the road near the old quarry and the car skids

across dirt. "All right!" he yells as he opens the door and jumps out; his voice hits the rocks and splits a thousand times. Grandpa never let me go here on my walks. "Wander where you like, Charlie, but the old quarry's dangerous. Loose rocks fall on you from nowhere."

"Woohoo!" Antony screams even louder.

In what world does arriving at a dark place full of rocks call for a woohoo? "Luke, I want to go home."

"Relax. Have a drink."

"I'm not thirsty."

"Not that sort of drink." He empties the can and reaches for another.

I look across at the car. I must be the only kid in this place above ten who can't drive. Please send someone to save me. It feels like we sit for hours. I hold my knees and wish as hard as I can on the star that's sitting on the horizon. All the while Antony and Luke are talking about how they're going back into town to do some damage; I'm watching that star on the horizon get closer. I've never seen one fall horizontally before.

"So, you ready to head back?" Antony asks, and his breath smells like rotten fruit. If he drives now, he'll kill us. "Make a decision, Charlie," Mum says, and she's right. I should make sure Dad doesn't get another phone call like the two others he's had.

Antony and Luke walk toward the car. I stand still. I've been trying so hard to fit in and do what everyone else is doing, but sometimes doing your own thing is fine. It's the finest thing there is. "I'm walking back," I say. They're too drunk to notice. I jog over to them. If they're too drunk to notice, then they're too drunk to drive.

I put my foot out a centimeter. Antony trips over it. I trip Luke, too, and he takes a little while to work out how the ground hit him. "And you call me Charlie Dorkin," I say, trying to decide on the next part of my plan. It doesn't go any further than this, though. Antony stands. I trip him again. It's going to be a long night, I think. But then that star gets close enough to make a little noise. Thank God. Stars don't grunt.

"Hey," Dave calls out, wobbling toward us on his bike. He gets off and looks at Luke and Antony on the ground. Antony stands. I trip him up. "I see you've got this under control," Dave says.

"I could do with a lift." You owe me that, at least. I walk over to his bike. He shakes his head, goes to the car, and bends behind the wheel. Is hot-wiring a car taught in schools here? I get in the front seat and Dave hits the accelerator.

We don't talk until he stops the car and kills the lights. "This where they took it from?"

"Yep."

"You shouldn't have gone with them, Charlie. Antony's an idiot."

No shit. "Maybe I went because I'm Charlie Dorkin, Dave. Charlie Dorkin, Charlie Dorkin." I sing a bit for him in case he's forgotten. "I heard it all."

"You heard wrong."

"There's really only one way to hear Dorkin."

"They were talking about what they used to call you."

"Nice."

"You never spoke to us. You sat up in that tree."

"Because you were calling me fucking Charlie Dorkin."

"You didn't know that. I tried to talk to you all the time, and then one summer you arrived with your Walkman on and that was it. You never took it off."

"I don't get why this summer's any different. I was still Walkman-wearing weirdo chick when Rose asked me to the river."

"I never said you were Walkman-wearing weirdo chick." He's laughing, but I'm not ready to laugh. "I don't know. I thought maybe Rose was playing a joke."

"I'm loving this brutal honesty."

"But I don't think that anymore. She wanted to rip Luke's head off tonight," he says.

"And you?" I ask, staring through the windshield at a sky naked of smog and city lights.

"You can't really think I've been hanging around you for a joke?" he asks, and I know what Gus meant when he said the air drummed. The world's drumming tonight. I wind down the window.

"I remember this time I saw you dancing with your mum," Dave says. "She was singing into a tomato sauce bottle and you were playing air guitar."

"I was eight." I'd been crying because I knew that Rose didn't want to go swimming with me. "Do I have to ask her?" she'd said to her mum out the front of the shop, and I knew she was talking about me.

"Charlie?" Mum had said as I walked back inside. I was so angry, and she was the first thing I saw to throw my voice at.

"Get away from me." I tried to walk past her to my room but she caught me.

"Some people aren't worth crying for, Charlie." We sat on the floor of the shop for a long time. I remember feeling so tired I couldn't move. And then she let me go and turned on the music.

"Mum, don't," I said. But she was so funny singing into that bottle, and the guitar solo started and she pointed at me and I let go. For a second or two I didn't care what the Rose Butlers of the world thought of me.

"That was the Christmas before she died."

"I bet it's been a while since you played the air guitar," Dave says, and laughs. I don't tell him that I think of that memory every time I play a song. The one thing I'm glad about is that I didn't let Mum go solo that day. Every time something humiliating happens to me, I hear her calling out in that stupid voice, "Air guitar, Charlie." I imagine her like she was that day, shaking her long hair down over both our faces, laughing loud enough to wake Dad from his afternoon nap.

"I reckon you just needed to get your balance. You were sort of like a car without a spoiler."

I have no idea what Dave's talking about, but I want him to keep going. "What's a spoiler?"

"It uses the wind to push the car down so it's got grip when it goes round corners. It'd fly right off the road without one."

"Well, flying's a good thing, though, when you're racing?"

"Flying's good if you're a plane. You fly when you're a car, you'll go off the road and explode. You got to have balance between speed and grip."

"You think I've got balance now?"

He grins. "Sometimes."

"I guess sometimes is better than never."

"So you're okay, then?" he asks as a torch shines through the window.

"Dave Robbie," the policeman says.

"Constable Ryan."

"What a surprise, stealing cars and driving without a license. And who do we have here?" He shifts the small spotlight onto my face.

And now, ladies and gentlemen, give it up for Charlie Duskin, the girl who just can't seem to get a break. She's about to sing her own rendition of the jailhouse blues.

Mr. Robbie and Grandpa arrive at the same time. "We're letting them off with a warning," Constable Ryan says. "They're lucky."

I don't feel lucky staring through the bars at Grandpa, who's still wearing his slippers. I'm not in as much trouble as I could have been, though, because Dave lied for me. He gave me a long, hard shut-up glare and told the police it was his idea. "Charlie was in the car trying to stop me."

I let him take the blame. I don't say anything, even when Mr. Robbie comes up close to Dave and twists the lobe of his ear round tight. "Don't worry, Bill," he says. "He's grounded for a bloody lifetime."

Grandpa doesn't say anything on the way to the car. He gets in and fastens his seat belt and then sits there, staring at the road. "Fasten your belt," he says, and I do, but he doesn't start the car.

"I kept thinking about all the things that could have happened," he says. "Car accident, getting lost. Worse."

Maybe it's not right, but I'm glad that he's frightened. I'm glad that he's here in his slippers, not driving yet because his hands won't stop shaking.

"From now on I want to know where you're going, who you're going with. I haven't told your father yet. He wasn't home when the police called."

I nod.

"I didn't think Dave was that sort of boy."

"He's not that sort of boy," I say. "I got in a car with Luke and Antony after they'd been drinking. I went to the quarry with them. I'm the idiot, not Dave."

"Why, Charlie?"

"I guess I was born one."

"Not why are you an idiot. Why did you get in the car?"

Because it was too late to say no. Because I'm tired of being on the outside. "Dad barely notices me," I say, which comes from nowhere and has nothing and everything to do with tonight.

"He still misses your mother."

"I miss her, too."

"It's a different kind of missing, though. You're trying to remember, and he's trying to forget."

"He's forgetting me along with her."

He taps on the steering wheel. "Give him time."

"It's been seven years."

"Maybe you should sing him your new song, 'Where the fuck is Dad?'" he hums, and starts the car.

"You should have seen Antony's face tonight when I tripped him up so he couldn't drive."

"That's my girl," Grandpa says, and laughs. I laugh, too, but then I remember Dave's ear twisting in his dad's hand and I stop.

Rose

"Dave, you whispering in my ear at six in the morning is not the way I want to wake up." I switch the phone to my other ear and turn on the lamp.

He whispers some more.

"Speak louder. I thought you said 'jail' for a second."

"I did say 'jail.' Charlie and I got caught returning the car Luke and Antony stole to get to the quarry."

"What?" My voice rises about ten decibels. "Dave? Are you there?"

"Sorry. Couldn't hear you. I think I'm deaf now."

"This isn't funny."

"There's a jail cell with 'Dave was here' scratched onto the wall. You don't have to tell me that."

"Your dad must be angry."

"He's taking it better than I thought. I'm only grounded till I'm sixty."

"Tell me you at least did something with Charlie before you went into lockdown."

"Very romantic, making out in a prison cell with a toilet in the corner and Constable Ryan looking on."

"I'll bring her to visit when the heat's off."

"She's pretty pissed at you, Rose. She thinks maybe you're being her friend as a joke." There's quiet, and I know Dave's scratching his head and searching around like he'll find the right words in the air. "This is the last time I'll ask," he says.

"It's not a joke," I tell him. "I'll go say I'm sorry."

"Check she didn't cop it from her old man, too."

"It's so typical that Luke and Antony are the only ones getting off without trouble."

"I don't know. I wouldn't want to wake up hung over at the quarry with my bike the only way to get home."

"God, Dave, I love you."

"I'm glad someone does," he says as his dad yells things I can't listen to and shouts at him to hang up.

Charlie

Grandpa and Dad are already moving around when I open my eyes. I lie in bed and listen to their background music. It's Grandpa who raises his voice first. "She's not fine, Joe. She's alone most of the time."

"She's got friends down here."

Grandpa snorts and I hold my breath, but he doesn't tell. "You're not around half the time, and when you are you're busy with the shop or sleeping. You don't spend any time with her, Joe."

"Dad, it's none of your business."

"She's my business. You're my business. Arabella would be turning in her grave at the way you're acting." Grandpa's voice is softer than I've ever heard it. "You couldn't have known, Joe."

I wait for one of them to speak. To tell me what that means. *You couldn't have known.* Possums run inside the roof. Grandpa tries to scare them out every now and then, but they're settled. "Don't talk about her," Dad says, and walks past my room. The door clicks sharp on his way out. The possums scuttle at the sound.

Grandpa didn't tell Dad about last night, and he didn't ground me, either. Cool, sure. But not entirely fair. "I did a bad thing. I let Dave take the blame," I say to Mum and Gran. "I went to jail."

They don't argue with me as I go about punishing myself this morning. I get the little trolley and use it to load boxes from the storeroom at the back of the kitchen.

Grandpa looks up from the accounts when I'm on my third trip for washing powder and soap and peas. He leans his head out to the empty shop. "Are we expecting a rush on people needing to get clean and eat peas?"

"You never know."

"It's a beautiful day. Rose has called five times."

"I have to stack shelves."

"For how long?"

"Forever. People come, they buy, I stack."

"Okay, Dante."

"Who?" I ask.

"Never mind."

"You could ground me."

"I've had about enough of punishment in this family," he says, looking back at the accounts.

"Do they add up?" I ask.

"They never add up, Charlie."

I go back to my peas. I've been stacking for an hour when Grandpa walks out of the kitchen. "Rose called again."

"Tell her I'm not in." I keep my eyes on the shelves.

"Or you could tell her yourself," Rose says.

I look up and she's standing behind Grandpa. "I'm not in."

"I just want to check you're okay," she says, and Grandpa leaves us alone.

"I got arrested," I tell her, and keep stacking.

"I know."

"I got Dave arrested."

"I know." She walks over and looks down at me. "I'm sorry about the camping trip, about you overhearing us."

"Charlie Dorkin, Charlie Dorkin," I sing quietly. "You must have really hated me."

"I didn't know you then. But you were always hiding up that tree, staring at us."

"Maybe I wanted to join in," I say.

"Maybe you should have asked."

"Would it have made a difference?" I look at her and she's thinking about it. She's actually thinking about it. "Get lost. I don't need people pretending to be my friend." I rip open a box of washing powder while she hovers. "I said get lost." She kneels beside me and stacks boxes.

"I'm not pretending," she says after a while. "You're funny. I never noticed that before."

I keep stacking.

"Dave says I've lived in this town too long." She lines up

164

labels. "Maybe I have. I wanted to meet different people so bad, and then when I met you I gave you shit because you were weird."

"Is that supposed to make me feel better?"

"I'm saying I like being your friend now."

"You're not saying it very well."

"Sometimes it feels like Luke and Dave don't hear me unless I'm talking about cars or sex or fish and chips. Mum doesn't hear me unless I'm saying something she agrees with. But you listen to me."

I rip open a box of toilet paper and we stack it together.

"I've been playing your music before I go to sleep. It makes me feel like there's something else other than plastic chairs out the front of a shop." She sits back and looks at the rows. "You plan on forgiving me?"

"I'll think about it after we've unpacked Grandpa's order. There's more toilet paper, washing powder, nappies, some canned beans. That's just to start."

She goes into the storeroom and fills up the trolley. We keep unpacking and stacking. "Last night was my fault. I'm sorry." She sits on her heels and looks at the neat piles of canned food and toilet paper and washing powder. "This place," she says. "Tell me there's somewhere other than here."

I look at her, staring at the shelves, shoulders slumped toward them. I look at the rows of peas all the same, sealed in tight. "There's somewhere other than here," I say.

Rose

I stack box after box of canned peas and toilet paper, and I see my life in those neat little piles. "This place," I say to Charlie. "Tell me there's somewhere other than here."

She doesn't tell me to have a little patience. She doesn't tell me I'll get the things I want when I'm older. She tells me what I want to hear and then says to sit outside. She makes me chips and says, "When you want something really bad that you might never have, then the only thing to do is eat chips. It's either that or chocolate." She brings some of that out, too.

She puts them on the table between us and says, "I get the last one, though. As long as we're friends, I get the last chip."

"Fair enough. Fight you for the last piece of chocolate, though."

We eat quietly, and then after a bit she says, "I think—and I'm not sure, but maybe—it's not entirely crazy to say that Dave might kind of like me."

I look at her. "Are you fucking kidding?"

"Okay, maybe it is crazy."

"No, I mean, are you fucking kidding? Of course he likes you."

"Maybe."

"Maybe? He breathes heavy when you're around. He either likes you or he's allergic to that truckload of aftershave he's started wearing."

She's laughing when her dad walks up the path. "Hey," Charlie calls. "Nice day."

He nods like some customer said it to him. He lets Charlie do what she wants not because he trusts her. It's because he doesn't notice her. I'm looking at a family photo that's been sliced through the middle, and she and her dad are on separate pieces. Maybe it happened when her mum was cut out of the picture. Maybe it was always that way.

Mum might yell half the time and not listen properly the other half, but if I said something like "Nice day" to her she'd do a dance. If she didn't answer, I'd say it again and again till she did. Charlie just shrugs but she doesn't do it like other people do. She resettles her skin. I look across at my house. Dad's at the mailbox. "Nice day," I call out.

"Sure is, Rosie," he says. "Lucky I'm working nights. I get to enjoy it."

I don't do it to be mean. I do it to show her what things

should be like. The sun's creeping over her and she shifts back into shade and closes her eyes.

"Is your dad always so quiet?" I ask.

"I guess."

"He's never really talked to you?" It's brutal, but brutal's what it is.

"Before Mum died, he was a different kind of quiet. Early-morning kind of quiet." She sits up and puts her toes in the sun. "I remember him teaching me how to make toast when I was about seven. I said, 'It's just toast, Dad,' and he put me on the counter. He said, 'It's never "just" with food. You take good ingredients, good bread. Don't be impatient, Charlotte. Toast till it's golden. Spread real butter right to the edges.'"

"That was good toast you made the other night," I say.

"He's one of the top ten chefs in Melbourne. He taught me right. I can't cook anything other than toast, though. We had this father and daughter day once. I think I was in Year Three or Four. Every kid had to make something for their dad. So I made these biscuits. I read the recipe and mixed the batter. I wanted them to be sweet, so I doubled the amount of sugar. Mum helped me put them in the oven.

"That morning when we were getting in the car, I tasted one and realized I'd used salt instead of sugar. Dad said he was excited about my present and I couldn't tell him. He got out of the car at school, and I said it real quick to Mum. She covered her mouth and tried not to laugh because she could see I was panicking. 'I'll fix it, Charlie.'

"So she came in with us. We did the father and daughter

things, and then it was time to give our gifts in front of every-one. Dad opened his, and I kept saying to Mum, 'He can't eat them. Do something.'

"She held me back while he opened the tin and ate one. The look on his face only lasted a second. Then he smiled and ate five biscuits. Mum and I had to leave the room because she was laughing so loud. 'He's eating them!' she kept scream-ing. 'He's eating them.' Mum had the best laugh. The sort that took you with it.

"On the way home she was still cracking up. Dad looked at me in the rearview mirror and said in his dead-serious voice, 'They were very good, Charlotte. I'm thinking of adding more salt to my recipe.'"

"You ever remind him of that day?" I ask.

"He doesn't like talking about her."

"So what do you talk about, since she died?"

She thinks about it and resettles her skin again. "Some-times we talk about the weather."

I push the chocolate across. "Last piece is yours," I say.

"Stay away from Charlie, Luke. I don't want you hassling her to steal again." I left the shop and came straight here. Talking to Charlie was like sitting in a summer storm. Sweet grass and wind and just cool enough to set my skin rising. I don't want Luke hurting her or telling her about the scholarship, which amounts to the same thing.

"I didn't hassle her. Taking stuff from your own dad isn't stealing."

"Crap, Luke. You used her, and you know it."

"You can talk," he says.

"It's different for me. I'm not using Charlie to get a packet of cigarettes. I'm not even using her. I might tell her about the scholarship, and I might not, but either way I'm her friend now."

"She's not yours, Rose," he says, and I feel the same way I did watching him with Andrea Cushifsky.

"What's that supposed to mean?"

"It means what I said."

People say such stupid things sometimes. "Are you going to tell her about the scholarship?"

"You think I'd wreck everything for you?"

"I don't know, Luke. I didn't think you'd almost kill Charlie. How stupid can you be, getting into that car with Antony when he's been drinking? You could have been killed as well."

"Like you'd care."

"Are you a complete dickhead? Of course I care."

"I'm sorry I'm not as smart as you are. Not everyone can have a scholarship."

"I didn't say you weren't smart. I said you were stupid."

"I guess I'm too dumb to see the difference."

If Luke and I keep yelling like this, we'll end up saying things we don't even mean. We'll rip each other apart. I'm mad at him, but it's because he's acting dangerous. He'll get hurt and I won't be here to stop him. I'll be in the city. "I don't think you should hang out with Antony anymore."

"Well, you don't get to choose my friends."

"It's either him or me, Luke." As soon as I say it, I want to snatch it back from the air. But it's out of my mouth with a life of its own.

Luke's cornered. His face is as pale and tiny as the day he kicked Dave through the goals on the footy field. "Then it's Antony."

"Then it's over," I say. But what I really want is for Luke to grab my hand and run with me to the river. I want what I had before, Luke standing up for me no matter what. I want him right up to the second I leave this town. "And you won't tell Charlie about the scholarship?"

"I don't care enough about it to tell her," he says, and walks away. So this is what water feels like, I think, the second before it can't hold on any longer. This is what it feels like, the second after it lets go.

Dad takes one look at me when I get home and says, "Rosie, put your walking boots on. We're going out for the afternoon."

"I'm too tired to walk."

"Five minutes," he says. "Move it."

He drives to my favorite spot, where the mountain looks as if it's been cut away from the rest of the hills around it. The surface is jagged and crumbling, and if you climb to the top where the water runs through, "you might be lucky enough to find fossils," Miss Cantrell told me in Year 7. I've never found one in all the years I've been coming here. "Most things don't leave evidence of themselves when they die, they just crumble away," she said. "But if they live near water, then there's a chance some tiny part of them will be etched into the earth."

"You read a lot of stuff, hey, Rosie?" Luke always says when I try to explain it to him. He looks for fossils when we come up here, though. He looks because he knows how bad I want to find something.

"So, everything all right?" Dad asks while we eat the food Mum's packed.

"Yep."

"Luke hasn't been round all that much lately. Everything okay with you two?" I nod and sift through tiny pebbles. "You know, when your mother left for overseas, I thought I'd lost her. She had to go but it killed me to see her leave."

"Me and Luke aren't you and Mum, Dad." Luke and I are over. It's time I cut my losses and moved on. No more looking after him. No more saving him. No more believing him when no one else does.

I know Dad wants to help, but it's too little too late. He should have come here with me years ago; he should have kept coming with me to see the sunrises.

"So, you okay to walk or do I have to carry you back?" Dad asks after a while.

"Nope," I say, standing up. "I can walk on my own."

I brush my jeans clean of grit before we leave. "Not taking any rocks with you?" he asks.

"No." All this time I've been coming to this place and there's no history here, at least nothing worth taking with me.

Charlie

Rose is quiet this week, but it doesn't feel as though I've done anything wrong. It's a different kind of quiet than the one that sat between Dahlia and me after Louise told her about the auditions. I kept trying to make things better by bringing her cake or inviting her over to my house for one of our old-time sleepovers. "Can Louise come?" she asked, and I took as long as I could to say yes so she knew I meant no.

Rose walks into the shop today and says we can visit Dave tonight. "Ask your grandpa if you can."

"Mr. Robbie won't like that, will he?"

"I said we should visit Dave. I didn't say anything about his dad."

"I don't want to get him in any more trouble."

"Dave's always in trouble with his dad," she says. "It's just the way it is."

I think about that on the way, about whether I'd rather have a dad like mine or Dave's. "What's your dad like?" I ask Rose as we're walking.

"He talks more than yours does. But he works a lot. He's pretty tired since he started at the mill. It's more Mum who won't let me do stuff. I wanted to go on exchange last year, and I thought maybe he'd let me, but she wouldn't even talk about it. She says if I'm not careful I'll wind up in trouble. I tell her if I'm not careful I'll wind up like her."

"You actually say that?"

"It pisses her right off." She stops to catch her breath. "Check out that sunset."

Pink runs down the world. "Have you ever heard someone play the cello?" I ask.

"I'm not sure. What's it sound like?"

"That sky."

She nods. "It makes me ache."

I know what she means. A long line of horn or a note sung low makes me feel the same way.

"Luke and I broke up."

"I'm sorry," I say, and her being quiet this week makes more sense.

She starts walking again. "I knew it was coming."

"I never broke up with a boy before. Mainly because I never went out with a boy before."

"You're lucky," she says. "It feels like shit and both of us wanted to end it. Imagine how I'd feel if he'd dumped me."

"It's not the same, but Dahlia stopped talking to me before I left."

"I thought you said she called all the time."

"She did call me other summers. Not this one, though. I acted stupid last year. I lied to her about stuff."

"How come?"

"I wanted her to think I was as good as Louise Spatula, this friend of hers who hates me."

Rose nods. She doesn't say anything till we reach the edge of Dave's property. "Louise Spatula is a stupid name," she says, and then we keep on walking.

Rose

"Dahlia stopped talking to me before I left," Charlie says. "I acted stupid last year. I lied to her about stuff." I cut her a break today and don't push her about it. I'm measuring out a little bit of brutal at a time. I tell her, "Louise Spatula is a stupid name." Everything about Louise is stupid if she doesn't like Charlie. I should know. It takes one to know one.

We get to Dave's and I tell Charlie to wait near the trees. I walk quietly along the side of the house till I get to Dave's window. I break off a branch and stretch it up to tap on the glass. Dave sticks his head out almost straightaway. "It's taken you long enough. I've been locked in here for weeks."

"It's been five days, Dave."

"It feels like weeks. Did you bring Charlie?" he asks, crawling out of his window.

I nod. "You heard Luke and I broke up?"

"Yeah. He came out to say sorry for getting me grounded."

"Luke said sorry?"

"He bought me a car magazine. Same thing."

Sometimes I wish I was a guy. Life's so much easier for them.

"So, Dave, are you planning on making a move tonight? Maybe asking Charlie on a date?"

"Maybe."

"By 'maybe' you mean you plan on staring at her and doing nothing?"

"I'm not sure she's interested."

"She laughs at every joke you make, and let's face it, you're not that funny. She listens to you talk about cars. She's been staring at you for nearly ten years. Make a move, Dave. Ask her out."

"You think she'd say yes?"

I make it as simple as I can. "She will say yes, Dave. But she won't if you don't ask."

We walk over to her hiding in the trees and Dave grins and she grins and I think if the two of them don't get on with it soon, they'll explode. They grin all the way to the river.

"Isn't that Luke?" Dave asks, pointing over to the trees at the edge of the water.

"Yep," I say. "And Antony Barellan. What does he see in that guy?"

"Who else has he got to hang out with, Rose? Let's go get him."

"You get him if you want. I'm going home." I walk away quickly so Dave can't talk me into anything. Luke chose Antony Barellan, so that's who he's stuck with.

"Rose!" Charlie calls, and runs after me. "Wait."

"I'm fine. You should stay. Maybe you could make your move tonight."

"I don't have moves."

"You've got plenty of moves." I look her up and down. "You just haven't used them yet."

I watch her and Dave for a second, almost touching but not quite, and it makes me feel like I did watching that sky. Because they're about to get what they want.

Charlie

We leave Luke and Antony and Rose behind and follow the river away from town. I've got that beat under my skin again tonight, only this time it's more Motown than disco. I've got Barry White in my blood and if I can't make a move when my blood's singing like him then there really is no hope.

"So how'd your dad take the news?" Dave asks.

"Grandpa didn't tell him."

"You sound disappointed. I wish . . ." He keeps talking, but I'm distracted by this small shape ahead of us in the dark.

"Who's that?"

"My dad," I say. I'd know his shadow anywhere.

We follow quietly. Dave doesn't ask why. I hold the hem of his T-shirt, and he guides me through the trees. I know where we're headed; I knew the second I saw him. I pull Dave back when we're close. Dad walks into the clearing where I swim.

He's a tiny figure at the water's edge. If it were anyone else, I'd think they were enjoying the scenery: the silver water and the belly moon. But it's not anyone. This isn't anyplace.

I should feel sad, I guess, watching him hurt on his own in the night while he remembers how Mum said she loved him here. How here they thought they'd last forever. I'm too angry for sad, though; I miss her like he does, and if he'd asked I would have sat with him, sat with the rocks and stones and water and the ghost of her.

But he doesn't want me. He takes off his shoes and socks and soaks his feet in the water. He picks up stones and skims them. He digs his hands into dirt, hoarding her up, hoarding what it felt like to be loved by her, what her voice sounded like, how she smelled. All the things I'm forgetting. Things I'm so thirsty for I could drink the river dry.

I lose track of time watching. When Dad finally leaves, I walk out of the clearing and sit next to the shape he left in the grass. "Come look at this," Dave says after a while.

I follow him, past where we were standing to watch Dad. Farther even than that. "Through here there's this spot where the trees cover everything. Too far from the road for head-lights," he says. "Even Luke and Rose freak out a little in here."

We step through and leave the world. I wait for my eyes to adjust, but they don't. I can't see my own skin. "How do you know about this place?"

"Heaps of spots like this in the bush. Some nights I wander on my own," he says. "Some nights me and Luke and Rose camp around here."

He's only voice now. Only breath. "So are you having a good summer?" he asks.

"Yeah, great. I liked the bit where I stole the cigarettes."

"And the bit where you got into the car with two drunken lunatics?" he asks.

"And the bit where I got you arrested and let you take the blame."

"I stole the car back. I was the one driving," he says, his words floating into mine; if I move at all, we'll be kissing, and I want to kiss, but I'm not sure where that leads to in here.

"You were only driving because I couldn't."

"You can't drive?" he asks.

"I'm only sixteen."

"So am I. We're old enough to have our learner's."

I'm nothing but aching now and I wonder if he's done this before and if I'm allowed to ask him that or if there are rules that I don't know. "Dave?"

"Yeah?"

"I haven't done this before much. At all, really. That is. If we're doing what I think we're doing. And not just, you know, standing in the dark."

He laughs, but I don't feel stupid. I feel electric because his lips feather mine when he moves. "Do you want to go back?"

"No," I tell him. "I want to stay like this. Exactly like this."

We hover. Lips feathering. Chests spinning crazy. Skin burning. After a while I take out my iPod and give one earpiece to him and keep the other for me. I put it on shuffle and voices swirl around us and it's the strangest feeling. I'm nowhere and somewhere at the same time. The last song we listen to is one of mine. He doesn't know it and I don't tell him. I feel stranger still. As if the singer and me are different people.

We walk home and he holds my hand and tells me about the car he's doing up at his job, about how the something or other connects with the thingumajiggy. I don't have a clue what he's talking about and I don't care as long as he keeps talking.

At my door he grins and says goodbye. He calls back from the gate, "Hey. Charlie. I haven't done it a whole lot, either."

"It feels like you have."

"Maybe I've just thought about it more than you," he says. There's no way I can sleep tonight, no point even trying. I grab my guitar and sit outside and close my eyes so the world is dark.

Wait a Little Longer

If you wait a little longer
I'll be getting closer soon
I'm really very close

So please don't move

Got some things to say
And you'll be hearing from me soon
I'm not that far away

So please don't move

I'm writing almost-love-songs
That I'll be singing to you soon
They're really close to ready

So please don't move

Charlie

Even in the early hours, I don't sleep. I get up at six and wait
in the kitchen for Dad. At seven he walks in, puts on the kettle,
and stares out the window while it boils. "Good morning,
Charlotte." He talks to his reflection.

"What friends did you visit last night?" I ask.

"Jessie and Tim Bell," he says without turning around.

"All night?"

"We talked till about one a.m., I think." He pours his coffee. "Did you and Grandpa watch a movie?"

"I hung out with Rose and Dave. We went to the river."

Dad faces me. I'm getting closer and closer to what I want
to say. Grandpa walks in. "Morning, you two. Summer storm

coming. It'll be here by tonight. Big one. Don't be out in it, Charlie."

"No, Grandpa."

"I'm off to get a part for the fridge," he says. "The thing isn't working properly. Something's off in the kitchen. Could one of you open the shop?"

"I will. Dad doesn't look like he's in the mood."

Rose

"So, what happened last night?" I ask, wandering round while Charlie counts the till. "Did you make your move on Dave?"

"Kind of," she says with her eyes on the money. "How did you and Luke get together?"

"He kissed me in Year Six. A hit-and-run in this game of chasey. My face was still burning when I got home. Mum thought I had flu. I waited two years for him to do it again."

"Were you nervous?"

"Did you hear me? I waited two years. It might have been nerves, but it felt more like desperation."

"So how did you get him to kiss you?"

"I think I said, 'You idiot. Kiss me.'"

"I was the one who didn't kiss last night," she says.

"I came close. The freaking cicadas were singing Barry White, and I couldn't do it."

"Who's Barry White?"

"Love god. I'll play him for you sometime," she says. "How do you get to that last bit?"

"Again, I say, two years."

"I've never kissed anyone, so it's been sixteen years for me."

I never had a problem going that last bit, but hearing that won't help her. "Maybe you ease into it," I say. "Take it a step at a time."

"That's what Dave said."

"Dave's a good guy."

"Dave's a great guy. Maybe I should just trip and land with my lips on his face."

"Yeah, but Dave doesn't usually get subtle," I say, and then we're doing that silent laughter thing, out of control at the thought of Charlie throwing Dave into the pool, her bikini top off and him still not getting it.

"Will you and Luke work it out?" she asks when we've settled.

I pick up a book of maps and flick through to one of the city. "I want to be as far away from him as possible, and when I'm away I wonder what he's doing."

"Do you go find him?" she asks.

"I don't need ESP to know half the time he's somewhere acting like an idiot."

"So why do you like him?"

"Because the other half of the time he's acting like Luke. He's making me laugh and wearing that sleeveless T-shirt."

"I was always jealous of the way he looked at you."

"I was always jealous of you leaving here at the end of the summer."

"You never really know what someone else is thinking," she says. I nod and put down the map.

Charlie

Rose leaves to babysit, and I look through some back issues of *Rolling Stone* that Gus lent me for the summer. I'm circling bands I wouldn't mind putting on Dave's compilation CD when Antony walks in.

He picks up things and puts them down, then picks them up again. He curves his head around to look at me and licks his lips. I sit behind the counter and keep circling bands, looking up occasionally to see if he's still in the store. He winds his way to the register until he's close enough to bite. "Can I help you?" I say.

"No one can help you." He laughs. He probably heard someone say that line on TV and has been waiting all his life to use it. He hates me, I see that. And yeah, maybe I could lie to myself and say it's because I tripped him up, but that's not true. He treats me the way he does because he can. Antony knew what sort of person I was as soon as he saw me sitting out the front of the milk bar. He picked me for someone he could use; if he can't do that anymore, then there's no reason to be nice. "Did you hear me?" he asks.

"I heard you." I keep leafing through my magazine.

"Something stinks in here," he says.

"Didn't smell before you walked in," I answer. It's an oldie but a goodie.

"Oh yeah?" he asks, which is old but not so good.

"Get out unless you're buying, Antony," Grandpa says, walking in the back way. It's the oldest and the best.

I'm smiling, feet up, reading my magazine when Dave arrives. "What are you doing?" he asks.

"I'm sitting here thinking I'm not entirely uncool."

"Will you be doing that all day? My dad's gone for the afternoon. Mum's given me time off for good behavior."

"What are you going to do with your time off?" I ask.

"Teach Charlie Duskin how to drive."

Driving looks so easy when someone else is doing it—you put your foot on the pedal, turn the wheel a bit, and sing with the radio. The only song I'm singing today is "Shit." Occasionally I mix it up with a rendition of "Fuck" from the start of summer.

"Shit. Fuck. Shit."

"Charlie, look out!" Dave yells as we jerk across the paddock. "The fence, shit, brake. Brake!"

"What foot?" I scream.

"The right!" He holds on to the side of the truck as we fly into the fence. "Your other right."

"Sorry, Dave."

"Don't worry about it," he says, twisting his neck around. "Just a bit of whiplash."

"I told you I wouldn't be able to do it."

"No one gets it the first time."

"Except for every kid in the country."

"You should see Luke behind the wheel. Stop giving yourself a hard time."

"Sorry."

"And stop saying sorry. I'd rather you told me get lost than sorry."

"Get lost, then," I say, and start the car. "I'm driving!" I yell after we've lapped the paddock three times. "I am driving. Do you think your dad'll be angry about the fence?"

"Do another lap. Let's put off telling him as long as possible."

If the day had a sound track, the main song would thump with a backbeat of laughter. It would be written and sung by Charlie Duskin. It would be loud.

But it wouldn't be as loud as Mr. Robbie when he gets back early. "What the bloody hell were you doing in the back paddock, anyway?" he yells, and I hate the way he spits words at Dave.

"Practicing my driving," Dave says.

"How did you hit the fence?"

"I got confused, between the accelerator and the brake."

"You'll have to pay for it. And you can spend this afternoon fixing it."

"Yep."

"You're an idiot, Dave."

"Yep."

"You haven't cut the grass in that paddock like I asked you, either. Snakes'll be crawling through it if you don't do it soon."

The whole time Mr. Robbie's shouting, digging with his voice, I hide like Dave said I should. I want to walk out there and tell him Dave wasn't the idiot, I was, and by the way, neither of us are idiots. While I'm out there, I want to yell that it wasn't Dave who stole the car, either. I come out of my hiding place too late, though. Mr. Robbie's gone.

"Go home, Charlie," Dave says, face bent against the wind that's starting now. "It'll rain soon. I have to fix the fence."

He slumps on the ground outside the barn, and I turn my back. His knees are pulled to his chin, and his head is down, and I walk away because that's what he told me to do. I stop at the gate, staring at the fence around Dave's yard. I hear Mum telling me to go back.

Dave's got his face to the wall when I sit next to him. He's half crying, half holding it in. "I said go home, Charlie. I don't want to talk about it."

"So don't talk," I say. And I hold his hand while he washes the last sixteen years out.

We sit there for ages. Dave's the first one to speak. "Your

dad's not much better than mine. How come he hardly talks to you?" He and Rose are the only ones who ever said it like that before, just like it is. "I guess he misses Mum. He doesn't talk much to anyone."

"When did she die?"

"When I was nine."

"That's a long time to be sad."

And maybe he's talking about me and maybe he's talking about Dad, or maybe he means both of us. It doesn't matter. All that matters is that someone else other than me is saying that something's wrong. More wrong than her dying.

I stare across the paddocks that seem to stretch forever. Dave grips my hand tighter because now it's my turn to cry. "I always wonder why some paddocks are green and some are dry when they're right next to each other," I say.

"Different things going on underneath," Dave explains. "Some have got better irrigation." It makes sense in a way I can't explain.

Charlie

"You don't have to help me fix this," Dave says, standing at the fence.

"I broke it. I'm fixing it."

"You have any idea how to mend a fence?" he asks.

"No. But I can learn."

"All right, go back to the truck and get me more nails. Put on the radio while you're there."

I switch on some music and turn it up loud. I can't find the nails. I look in the rearview mirror to see if Dave's close enough to yell to, but he's lost in the long grass. From where I'm standing, I'm completely alone in a sea of burnt green.

"Charlie, hurry up!" Dave yells across the paddock.

"I'm coming. I can't find the nails."

"Charlie," he calls again, and this time I hear it properly, a black blanket that spreads over the day.

"Dave?" My voice rises with every step. "Dave?" My feet trip, and I fall on the ground next to him.

"Charlie, calm down." He smiles, sweat forming glass circles on his white skin. "I'm fine. Remember, panic is bad for a snakebite victim."

"Snakebite. Shit. Should I suck the poison out?"

"Remember, panic is bad. Start the truck and drive me to the house. It'll be easier for you to go out the side gate and come around by the road."

"I don't have a license."

"You're willing to cut me and suck the poison out of my blood, but you won't drive on the road without a license?" he asks, and pulls himself up on my shoulder. "You're crazy."

"You're a little slow if you're just working that one out," I say, but neither of us laughs.

I haul Dave across the field and into the truck. My shoulders ache, but I can't stop. His voice fades as his body gets heavier, dragging me under where I don't want to go. I'm drowning under the weight of him, ice-cold in the heat of the day.

"Turn the ignition, Charlie," he says. "Start the engine." It won't work. "Dave, it won't go. Dave?" The birds are screaming overhead. I turn the key and put my foot flat on the pedal, but there's nothing. I'm doing everything I did before, but it's dead. Even then I know it's too late. I keep my foot flat on the pedal till Dave's face turns the color of clouds. That's when I realize: there are no birds. Only me, screaming for help. And Dave, quiet as death.

"Stop being so scared all the time!" Dahlia yelled the week before Jeremy's party. "Join a band. Talk to people. Stop acting like I'm doing something wrong because I'm hanging out with Louise."

She's right. I need to stop being so scared of things ending and do something to make them start. I know how to do this. I learned it in school. I put the seat back. I make sure Dave's airway's clear. I give him mouth-to-mouth and check his pulse. It's a shaking bird beneath his neck. "Thank God. Thank God. Thank God." I rip the sleeve off my shirt and wrap the cloth around his arm. I find some rope in the truck, grab a rock, and tie it to the horn so sound blares across the paddock. And I run. I run faster than I have ever done before, jerking and heaving through the grass. Dave's brother meets me halfway across the paddock.

"Snakebite!" explodes from my mouth, but I don't stop. I keep running to the phone. He runs to Dave.

Charlie

Mr. Robbie walks straight past Luke and me as though we're not here. I'm glad Luke is; he can be a witness if Dave's dad finishes the snake's job. "I told you to cut that grass," he says.

Luke pulls me out the door. We listen to their conversation from two chairs in the hallway. "I knew his dad gave him a hard time, but not like that," Luke says, swinging one leg. "Dave can hardly talk, and the first thing he does is yell at him."

"He's scared," I say. I smelled it in the sweat of his shirt as he walked past me.

"I don't care," Luke says. "I reckon Dave's scared, too."

Mr. Robbie stops talking, and so do we. Luke stares at the floor the whole time. He's the first one to break the quiet. "Does Rose even miss me?"

"I think so. Maybe you should ask her."

He shakes his head and keeps looking down. "You know, you can see yourself in this floor," he says, and walks off, leaving me on my own in the corridor. I don't feel on my own, though. I look into the shine of the floor and see someone who's got more of a clue than she did yesterday. Mr. Robbie walks out to talk to the nurse. "You," he says to me on the way past, "bloody flooded the engine, didn't you?" I smile.

He's so relieved, he's been crying. He just doesn't know the right way to say it. I guess there are a lot of people who don't know the right thing to say. You don't notice them so much because they pretend they do. Mr. Robbie should tell Dave that he loves him; he knows that. It's like he can see the word on the floor but it's slippery and awkward and he can't get a grip on it.

Mrs. Robbie rushes in and grabs it straightaway. "Dave, I wasn't home, I just got the message, thank God. . . ." She runs all her words together as she presses her face against his and grabs his hand.

Take a good look, Mr. Robbie. That's how it's done.

Rose

I've finally got my cousins off to sleep when Jenny from the caravan park rings the doorbell. "Your mum sent me, love. Dave Robbie's been bitten by a snake."

"Is he okay?"

"All we heard was he's at the hospital. I'll stay here. Your mum says ride your bike down there straightaway."

The hospital's at the edge of the freeway; I take every shortcut, and I'm glad I'm riding so fast because it means I can't think of what's waiting ahead. Luke's outside when I get there. "Is he okay?"

"Snakebite. But they got him here in time."

I feel sick from riding and relief. I sit on the grass, taking deep breaths. "Jelly legs," I say to Luke.

He turns his back and unlocks his bike. "You can visit. Charlie's in there, too. She saved him. You better ask her soon. Doesn't look like she needs you anymore." I watch him ride away.

And then there's just me and a few ambulances and a sky that's about to cave. I sit there waiting for my legs to stop shaking. Charlie walks out of the hospital. "He's okay," she says a few times before I really hear it.

"Luke said you saved him."

"I gave him mouth-to-mouth."

"Shame he was unconscious," I tell her, and she laughs.

"I thought he was going to die. I really thought it." We sit there thinking about a world without Dave.

"Thank God you were there."

"Thank God I was." She lies back on the grass and flings her arms wide. Like she can do what she wants without asking someone first. I lie back, too. After a while she dances her hands around in the air and says, "We're all major chords." We lie there a bit longer, thinking about that.

"The start of the summer feels ages ago," I say. "I miss Luke," I say. "You're a legend for saving Dave," I say.

"I am not entirely unlegend-like." She drums a little more at the air. "I'm calling it. I'm an absolute legend."

"I have to talk to you later, about something important."

"About Luke?" she asks.

"About Luke and this place. About me. Meet me at the river after dinner."

"Are you okay?"

I nod, and we stare at the sky a little longer. "You notice how the moon's been coming out earlier and earlier lately? Like it's saying, 'Fuck the rules. I'm here.'"

"It must have something to do with the sun, though," she says. "It doesn't have light of its own, does it?"

"The moon's got its own thing going on," I say. "Cool and mysterious."

She stares at it. "So it has."

I get this feeling. Everything's about to start.

Charlie

I lie there playing major chords in the air below a cool and mysterious moon. I think about my next move. Mr. Robbie walks past. "Hey," I call. "Can I have a ride?"

"Brave," Rose says.

"See you at the river." I run over to the truck.

He starts the engine, and we sit side by side, and it's a different type of quiet again. It's the quiet you get when you don't know someone at all and you don't have anything to lose by not talking. Dad and I sit in a different kind of quiet.

I have to find Dad and tell him what I did today. I have to grab him by the shoulders and shake him. Shake him till he sees how I need him and how things between us have to change or what we've got will be dead.

I let myself imagine for a second what life would have been like if Dave had died today. I'd have to spend the rest of my life knowing that if I'd done things differently, I could have saved him. I'd have to bury today so deep that I'd never think about it again. It'd come back, though. It'd come back every time I liked someone or kissed them. It'd cover me in guilt every time I came back here.

I watch the patchy paddocks move past the window and they match up to make a picture but I can't quite see what it is. Mr. Robbie stops outside the milk bar. "Thanks," I say.

"Thank you," he answers, and there's something about love buried in his words. Before I get out, I tell him, "I stole the car. Dave was bringing it back so I wouldn't get in trouble. I broke the fence, too." I wave and shut the door.

Rose

Mrs. Wesson walks out of my front door as I'm about to walk in. I haven't seen her since the last day of school. What she says is "Hello, Rose."

What I hear is "Busted."

"When did you get back?"

"It's good to see you, too, Rose. I arrived home today. Now, I've got a question for you. Were you even going to tell them?"

"I was waiting for the right moment."

"That moment has long passed. I might have been able to help, if you'd let me." She nods back at the door. "Your parents are waiting."

Mum starts as soon as she sees me. "You are grounded.

You are grounded until you're old and your teeth are sitting in a glass next to your bed and you're wearing scuba suit underwear. And then, if I'm not dead, you're grounded some more." Anger sets fire to her skin. "You lied to us. Flat out lied!" she yells. "What were you planning on doing, running away and paying for the fees yourself?"

"It's a scholarship," I say.

"I know what it is. Mrs. Wesson told us. What I want to know is why *you* didn't."

"I tried. I asked if I could go on exchange. You were too busy cutting fucking carrots to listen properly. I asked about the scholarship and you wouldn't even talk about it."

"Don't you fucking swear at me. I'm not stupid, Rose. That day at the caravan park was after you'd lied and cut school. Go to your room. Stay there till I call you out."

"I won't go to my room!" I yell. "I'm going to that school. It's got the best science program in the state and I got in and I'm glad because it means I won't be you, working my arse off at some shitty job."

"That shitty job pays for your food."

"Fuck you. I hang out the washing. I cook dinner when you're working. I look after your sister's kids."

"That's enough, Rose," Dad says.

But it's not enough. It's the best feeling, yelling at her, smashing the air with things I've been thinking for years. "You work all the time. You don't even read the paper anymore. I have nightmares where I end up like you. Pregnant and stuck here."

Mum holds the back of the chair. Dad's mouth is a circle. "I want to leave with Charlie at the end of the summer. I want to live with her and Mr. Duskin and go to school in Melbourne."

Mum leans her head against her hand. "You won't be going with Charlie at the end of the summer. I rang Mr. Duskin to make sure he knew that you two might be planning something."

"What did you tell him?"

"The truth. That you'd known about this scholarship since before school ended, that I thought you were desperate enough to do anything to get away."

Her words sink in. I taste metal. "Don't you get what you've done? Charlie will think I used her."

"From what I can see you did use her, Rose. Take a good look at yourself. If she's hurt, there's one person to blame."

"You had no right to tell her."

"I had every right. I'm your mother."

"Well, I always said Charlie Duskin was lucky."

Mum walks into the kitchen. I walk out the front door. Through the living room window, I see Dad standing with his hands held out in front of him as though he were holding something that suddenly disappeared.

Charlie

Dad's sitting in the kitchen in front of a chocolate cake and a pot of tea when I get home. He's heard. Mrs. Butler must have told him that I saved Dave, and he's baked a cake to celebrate.

"Did Mrs. Butler ring?"

He nods, and I'm waiting for him to say he's proud. When he does that, I'll tell him how much I miss him. I'll bring him back from wherever it is he's been. "She's worried about Rose, Charlotte. If you know anything, you have to tell me."

"What are you talking about?"

"Rose's parents know about the scholarship. They know she's been planning to leave at the end of the summer. Has she mentioned anything to you about running away?"

"No," I say, and I finally hear the chord that's been missing from our friendship. C-sharp. Cats cry in that note, lonely late-at-night calls, hungry for company. "Of course," I say, more to myself than him.

"Of course what, Charlotte?"

"She didn't tell me." I want him to understand why this is so terrible, but he can't because he doesn't know me. He sits there looking through those tiny square glasses, and I feel my anger rising like blood from a cut deep as bone. It's taken seven years to get to the surface, but now it's spreading out, over Rose, over him. "Don't you get it, Dad? She was using me so she could move to the city. Hang out with Charlie Dorkin, be nice to her, and she'll ask her dad if you can go with them at the end of the summer."

"Charlotte, calm down. You don't need friends like that."

The song we've been singing switches from acoustic to electric. I write loud, angry chords on the spot and send them out to him. "How would you know what I need? You never ask me. Did you know Dahlia doesn't talk to me anymore? She got sick of me because I sit at the edges and I don't do anything."

"What are you talking about? Dahlia's your best friend."

"She hasn't rung me once since I've been here. Haven't you noticed? I don't blame her, either. I let people walk over me. I lie rather than sing at a school concert, when I could blow those guys away."

"Of course you could blow them away."

"How would you know? Gus knows more about me than you."

"Is that why you stole the cigarettes? To get my attention?"

I think back to Dad watching me cry, to needing his help and not getting it. Unbelievable. Fucking unbelievable. "Why didn't you stop me? Dave's dad would have grounded him for a week."

"You want me to be like Mr. Robbie?"

"I want you to be someone."

He doesn't speak, so I yell. "What's the point of anything if all you do is think about Mum? You might as well be dead, too."

We're on opposite sides of the table waiting for the next thing to happen. Neither of us knows what that is. Dad gets up and walks out like he always does. "What, no money?" I ask. He keeps moving to his room.

That's okay. Dad and I have always been the quiet ones. Mum was the talker. She's dead, and she talks more than we do. I walk into my room. I stare at all the things Dad hasn't said to me over the years. CD after CD after CD. I open a bag and put in as many as I can fit.

I walk down the hallway to his room. I stare at him through the open door. I put the bag down and pick up the first CD. I make sure he's looking at me and then I take the disc out of the case and snap it. It sounds clean and sharp. I like it. I pick up the next one. *Snap*. I like that even more. I like the next and the next and the next even better. "Still nothing to say, Dad?" I ask. He's sitting on the bed looking confused as music cracks in my hands. "Why are you so sad?" He doesn't answer.

Some things take time. I walk to my room and click the clasps on my guitar case. I peel back the lid and take my voice out and walk down the hallway. Dad's still sitting on his bed, staring at the things broken around him. "What's wrong with you?" I ask. "What couldn't you have known?"

"Charlotte, you need to calm down." But that's not what I need. I raise my guitar high over my head. I hold it there, and it feels good to be doing something. I let go. I smash it toward the floor. I don't see Dad move. I feel the weight of him on the end, catching the body before it hits the ground. I let go and he sits on the bed, holding my guitar. Holding it tight. Rocking a little. And I'm not mad at him for not talking anymore. Some things are better than words. "I'll be back soon," I say. "There's something I have to do." He keeps holding my guitar and nods.

I'm not angry at all anymore really. I'm not sad. I'm certain. I take the road that leads to the river. Sunset sounds hard tonight, like heavy chords coming from the sky. Heavy chords that say the player's in control of the song.

"Charlie!" Rose calls as I walk toward her. The rain's been gathering in the air all day, and its arms are heavy with water. Any second it'll throw them open and soak us. Rose is a shadow in the half dark.

"You were lying all along." My disappointment feels like salty ocean in my veins, but I can swim.

"I'm sorry, Charlie."

"I told you things about Dave, about me."

"Dave doesn't know."

"I know Dave doesn't know. This is all you. How long were

you going to keep lying? Until you found someone in the city better than me who'd let you stay with them?"

"No. I wanted to stay with you." Her hands beat at the air, getting faster as she talks. "The scholarship's not the reason I wanted to be friends."

"Even if that's true, it's too late now."

"I don't care anymore. Tell me how to fix things."

"I don't want to fix things with you. You're not coming with us," I tell her, and it feels good to walk away.

"I only lied at the beginning," she calls. I take a last look back. The sky opens its arms and throws out the storm like old soapy water it's used and finished with. She's soaked and alone. I leave her huddled there. Some people aren't worth crying over.

Rose

Charlie's eyes aren't hollow anymore. They're rough and wide. "I don't want to fix things with you," she says, and I'm a hundred meters in the air with nothing below me. Rain hammers. She goes so fast she could be flying. My legs are stuck in mud, caught by all the dirt and dust in this place that's been gathering for ages, set free by the storm. "Fuck this town!" I yell to no one and the sky cracks again and the water pours so hard I can't see.

I climb into the old tree at the river. I hear Luke and Antony before I see them. I move as far as I can up the branches, and they hunker down beneath me where it's dry. Every muscle in my body works to hold me steady.

"It's pissing down," Luke says. "We should make a run for it."

"It'll ease in a bit," Antony answers.

They talk for ages without knowing I'm here. Luke says stuff like "Did you see Ferro hit that six on the weekend?"

And Antony answers, "Who do you reckon will win the next match?" It's not the most exciting conversation in the world, but even if I could leave, I wouldn't.

I want to fall down on Antony and push him to the side. I want to turn to Luke and tell him he really needs to get his hair cut a bit shorter at the back because it's sticking up. I want to tell him important things, too, like I can remember stealing bricks from the place next to mine because I wanted to build a fence around the bottom of our tree house.

Mum caught us and I told her it was all my idea so Dave wouldn't get into trouble. She didn't believe us, though, and she must have been real mad because she called Mrs. Robbie and Mrs. Holly. Dave's dad came and hauled him into the car and I could tell Mum felt guilty because she let Luke and me go to the river. We sat together under this tree and I made all these big plans to run away and Luke didn't say it was my fault that Dave was in trouble. He let me talk and then took me to his house and his mum made us hamburgers.

"You and Rose getting back together?" Antony asks as the rain eases and settles into a mist. Drops from me hit Luke, but he doesn't notice. "Not if you paid me," he says, and the two of them leave. I slide out of the tree and scratch my legs on the way down. I run home. I need to get inside and close that door.

Mum and Dad are sitting on the couch, looking at a book. I want to say, I remember that. I remember how we read together about places far away.

"It's the land of the midnight sun." Mum'd point at the picture. It sounded so romantic, like impossible things could happen to people there. She made me feel like things could happen to me. I want to say, I remember other things, too. How Dad kept a chart on the fridge with all my assignments on it, big crosses marked out when I handed something in. He always put my grade next to it, even when it wasn't good. "That's my girl, Rosie," he'd say. I want to ask them why they stopped. Why everything fun seemed to stop. I stand in front of them, dripping. They look up, and I get the feeling I could run my hands through both of them.

I go into my room and close the door. I imagine Dave's face when Charlie tells him what I did. I hear Luke's voice. *Not if you paid me.* I look at the protistans and play Charlie's music. That voice spins out again, and I think of those silkworms in their cocoons and how sad I felt when Mum said I wouldn't see inside. I never told her how one day I took one and boiled it. I cried so hard after it was done. I didn't know I'd feel like that. I just wanted so bad to touch the silk.

Charlie

I run home, arms open, face up to catch the rain. I shake the water off on the porch and go take a shower to heat my freezing skin. I call Dahlia. "It's Charlie."

"I know who it is. What do you want?"

A whole lot of things. "I'm calling to see how your summer's going."

"Good."

If a person hadn't been there all the time when I was lying and treating Dahlia like she belonged to me, they might think she was being harsh. But I was there. I couldn't lose her like I lost everything else, so without a word I made her feel bad for spending time with Louise. I planned sleepovers on nights when I knew there'd be parties, and I made her choose between new friends and me. I made her stand up for me instead of standing up for myself. She ignored me that day at Jeremy's party because I wouldn't say something to Louise and she was sick of me acting that way.

I keep talking and hope that sometime in the conversation we shift into who we were before things became like that. "So my summer's good, too. Kind of good. Strange, actually. I gave Dave Robbie mouth-to-mouth resuscitation after a snake bit him."

"Shit." She thinks about that for a second more. "Shit."

"I know."

"That's practically a kiss. You've practically kissed him."

"I almost kissed him for real. At night when we were walking by the river. We danced to some songs on my iPod. He didn't know it, but one of them was mine, the song I wrote, that time you stayed over."

"The one about sex?"

"It was never about sex, Dahlia; I told you that at the time."

"It was definitely about sex." Her voice is muffled, and I know she's pulled the phone into the hall closet to talk where her parents can't hear. "I kissed Jack Baker last week," she says. "It was bad. I kept thinking, Is it this bad because I'm bad or is he bad or are we both bad together?"

"Maybe you have to practice."

She thinks about that. "Better than practicing the piano, I guess. What else is going on? Is Rose still a bitch?"

"No more than Louise."

She doesn't answer for a second or two. "You should have told her she was a bitch at the party."

I stare out the window at the tangled garden. "I know. I think I'll spend less time with her next year. Maybe more time with Andrew Moshdon and some kids from music."

"Maybe audition for the final concert?"

"Maybe. I might try to get a band together. I'm singing at the local talent quest this Saturday." Until that second I hadn't decided.

"That's so cool."

I hear her walking out of the closet and into the kitchen. "What are you eating?" I ask.

"It's hard to say. Mum's been baking. I need your dad here to cook for me." She chews some more. "Or does hanging with Louise less mean you're cutting me, too?"

"We'll work it out. We're in Year Eleven. The in-crowd shouldn't matter so much."

"I don't like Louise because she's the in-crowd. I like her because I like her. I wasn't mad at you because you weren't part of the in-crowd."

"I know."

"Do you know?" she asks, and I can see her standing there like she did that day when those guys called us losers.

"I do." Some things take a while to know, that's all. "You want to hear my song about Dave and me?"

"Yeah. Just hold on a sec. Mum's asking when you're coming home."

"Tell her soon." And I play the first chord.

In my dreams tonight, the breeze is Mum's hair tickling my skin. But when I open my eyes, Dad's sitting on the chair near my window. "Is it morning?" I ask, blinking sleep away.

"Not quite, Charlotte."

The blue and silver light and the softness of his voice make me feel like I might still be asleep. "I dreamed of Mum," I say, and wonder if I'm talking about a dream in a dream.

"I do that all the time," he says. "Especially here." He looks at my guitar. "She says, 'Can you believe we made a daughter who sings like that?' I have to say that I never heard."

I get up, and my feet wobble on the way over like feet do when you walk after sleeping. I take the guitar and sit next to him in the blue light. There's honey on the air, set free from the jasmine by the storm. I play one of my songs. He taps his foot while I strum, and I feel like things might be changing, so I add an extra verse.

"So beautiful, Charlotte," he says.

"What's the bag for?" I ask.

"I'm going camping one last time."

"I'm singing at the talent quest on Saturday."

He looks at me, at my guitar. "I'll be there, Charlotte," he says, and walks out, leaving the door open. He comes back after five minutes. "Charlotte, if Dave Robbie visits again, leave the door like that."

"Sure thing, Dad."

Close to How

You're a ghost now
Falling
Through the dark
Trapped in rocks and dirt and water
You're a ghost now
And when I ask you why
You say sometimes death don't let us die

Sometimes life won't turn out like we want it
Sometimes life won't turn out like we want

He's a ghost now
Living
In the dark
Trapped by rocks and dirt and water
He's a ghost now
And when I ask you why
You say sometimes death don't let us by

Sometimes life won't turn out like we want it
Sometimes life won't turn out like we want

But sometimes in the honey night
Blue voice sweet and circling high
You forget the rocks and dirt and water
While you sing softly to the sky

Sometimes life turns out close to how we want it
Sometimes life turns out close to how we want

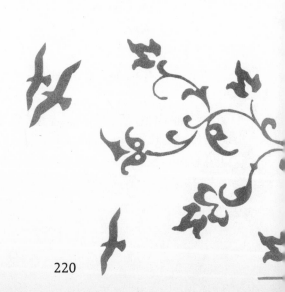

Charlie

Luke and I sit at separate tables outside the shop. He turned up for lunch a couple of hours ago and never left. He's turned up most days this week and sat staring at the hills. "What are you writing?" he asks today.

"Some lyrics for a song about this place." It's not the one I'm singing for the show; it's about him and Rose, but I don't say that.

"Must be a pretty quick song," he says. "About this place."

I give him a laugh because he looks like he needs it. "Have you seen Dave today?"

"This morning. That scary nurse with the mustache kicked me out."

"I'm visiting this afternoon if you want to go together. Two against one scary nurse with a mustache."

"Yeah, okay. Not sure two'll be enough. It's a big mustache." He keeps staring at the hills. "Dave'll be unbearable when you leave. He goes on and on about you. It's like being hit by a cricket bat. No offense."

"None taken."

His eyes stay on those hills, even though he can't see Rose from here. "You're not taking her with you?"

I shake my head. "She's staying."

"She's not staying," he says, kicking at the dirt. "Even if she stays, she's not staying. Her mum and dad did it in the back of a car, you know? Had her when they were young."

"I didn't know that."

"A Holden. Good car. I think maybe that's why she wouldn't do it with me. Didn't want that to happen to her. I wouldn't care about not doing it with her, if she'd get back together with me," he says.

A yellow car drives past the shop, and I watch it go. The day's a hazy blue. "That's where Rose used to sit," Luke says. "Right where you're sitting." A fly lands on the table and doesn't move. "I know," I say, staring at it. I imagine day after day of sitting here.

"I'm bored to death," Luke says, and I nod. Like Gus told me, you don't always understand people, so you gotta understand yourself. Then maybe you take what you worked out about yourself and use it to figure out other people.

"I want things, too," Luke says.

"Like what?" I ask, even though I get the feeling he's not talking to me.

"I don't know what. But that doesn't mean I don't want them."

Antony rides over and stands in front of us. "Shit, things must be quiet."

"Shut up, Antony," Luke says. "I'm talking to Charlie."

There is something kind of likable about him. "You want some free chips?"

He grins. "Yeah. Thanks."

"What about me?" Antony asks.

"She doesn't give everyone their chips for free," Luke says.

I ride on Luke's handlebars to get to the hospital. "You should bring your bike down next Christmas," he says.

"I'm asking Dad to buy me one for my birthday," I tell him, and he goes through what I should buy and how much I should pay.

He's still going on about it when we walk into Dave's room. "Charlie's getting a bike for her birthday. I said a hybrid's better because she can ride in the city and country."

"No more riding on people's handlebars?" Dave asks.

"Nope. I'm taking to the road."

"Better wear a helmet."

"This jelly is shit," Luke says.

Dave throws a magazine at him. "I was saving that."

Luke throws it back, and the nurse walks in and tells us to

be quiet. "She's why women should shave," Luke says. "Close shave."

"It's the new millennium," Dave says. "They don't have to shave."

"I think the venom went to your brain," Luke answers. "It's making you hallucinate and think that you're Rose. You'll be trying to kiss me next and then calling me a dickhead after you're done."

"The venom of fifty snakes could not make me hallucinate enough to kiss you. But you are a dickhead."

Luke turns on the TV.

"So I'll be well enough to go to the talent quest Saturday," Dave says. "You're going, right, Charlie? We should all go together."

"I'll meet you there. I'm going with Grandpa. With Dad, too, if he's back in time."

"Something special you're doing before you leave?" he asks.

"Yeah," I say. "Something special."

Luke goes, but I stay awhile longer. I watch Dave sleep and do a little writing and thinking. Hospitals used to remind me of Mum. Not because I'd ever seen her in one. I imagined her there, though. I imagined her being rushed in and saved. I imagined that over and over in the month after she'd gone. I didn't play music. I imagined that moment.

And then Mum's friend Celia mailed me that Stones album we danced to. I remember that summer Dave talked about, the one when I started wearing my Walkman. I remember because I'd worked out how good it felt to block the world. I even wore it sometimes at dinner with Dad. He made a little sign when he wanted me to pass the salt.

"What are you doing?" Dave asks, opening his eyes.

"I'm sitting here thinking about dead people."

"I like how you come in here to cheer me up."

"I like it, too." I pass him some water.

"I keep having this dream about snakes," he says.

"That's normal."

"The snakes are wearing little hats."

"Okay, that's not so normal."

He takes a sip and thinks for a bit. "What's normal?" The snakebite victim high on painkillers makes a really good point. "Stop thinking about dead people," he says, and drifts back to sleep.

I take the advice of the snakebite victim high on painkillers, since he seems to be making sense. I make a New Year's resolution list. It's not one of those I'll-be-good lists. It's a list of killer things coming up this year. I don't have to think all that hard to write it. I let the good stuff fall on out of me.

Finishing my song for Saturday, standing up there and letting it roll out and hit the audience, hit them and vibrate on their skin. Giving Dave his CD before I go home. Kissing him and having the stars go harmonic. Heading back to the city in the early morning, sun raining pink. Stopping at the gas station and stocking up on candy for the trip home. Sharing some with Dad and playing him some tunes I think he might like. Telling Dahlia about the summer and not telling Louise to get stuffed because, really, who cares about her? Calling Andrew and asking him to meet me out the front of school on the first day of Year 11. Lying in the sun in the quad on the last days of summer. Studying music. Getting a band together. Paying Beth to give me real singing lessons. Working and waiting for new releases that can be mine before anyone else's. Sitting with Gus and talking about musicians who are the biz. Seeing bands. Singing.

I stop writing when the nurse comes in. "He goes home Saturday morning," she says. I make "keeping out of hospitals" the last thing on my list.

I pass Rose on my way out. She's locking up her bike, so she doesn't see me. I don't call to her. I walk across the grass, over the spot where we talked the day I saved Dave. I get this feeling, an instinct. She wasn't lying to me then. I think a few good thoughts about her and keep on my way.

The End of Her

She's sitting on the hill
Hoping for a day
When her dreams don't hit the road
She's throwing rocks and yelling
At the sky and at the weather
She's yelling at forever
That's been breathing on her neck

She can't start with him again
He's got the end of her
He can't give her ocean
And he can't give her her

He's staring where she sat
It's the plastic that reminds him
Of something that they had
He says, "I'd give up sex forever
If she'd say we're back together"
But he's making promises he knows
It'd kill them both to keep

She can't start with him again
He's got the end of her
He can't give her ocean
And he can't give her her

Rose

I've watched Luke and Charlie sitting together most days this week. I watched them ride off along the street this afternoon and tip over in front of my house. It's the first laugh I've had in a while. I would've paid money to talk to either of them. I haven't had the guts to call Charlie since the river. I want to. I want to tell her and Luke that my house is a ghost town. Tufts of people rolling past. I'm grounded, but sometimes Mum says without looking at me, "Go out, Rosie. Just go out."

I don't sit at the freeway. It makes me think of old blue Fords and falling protistans and the things I did and the things I can't have. I hate that Mum's not talking to me, and I hate that Charlie and Luke aren't talking to me, either, and I hate that even though I hurt people it doesn't change that I want to get out of this place. Everything's tangled inside.

Luke's hanging around the shop late this afternoon, so I figure it'll be all clear at the hospital. Most days I ride toward there and then ride back, because I'm sure Charlie's told Dave, and I don't want to hear all the things he'll say. I get home and think it'd be better to hear something than nothing, so I ride out again and then stop halfway and come home. Today I ride all the way.

I sit on the edge of his bed trying to talk about something other than Charlie or Luke or the scholarship. "You're quiet," he says.

"Nothing ever happens here, so there's nothing to talk about."

"What's up with you?"

"I'm grounded," I say, just to say something real. "I told Mum to fuck off."

He whistles. "Why'd you tell her that? Any other 'off' leaves room for parole. 'Sod off,' 'shove off'—even 'sock off' is still pretty satisfying."

"You've told your dad to sock off?"

"Once. He said, 'What the fuck is "sock off"? Be a man and tell me to fuck off.'"

"So did you tell him?"

"No. Because that was the trap. There's never time out for good behavior with 'fuck off.'"

"Is your dad better since the accident?"

He nods. "People keep calling it an accident. That snake bit me on purpose. I've named it Sneaky. Sneaky had it all planned. I saw its face."

"Maybe it was hungry," I say.

"You're standing up for the snake?" he asks.

"No." I'm not standing up for the snake. "Hungry isn't a defense."

He laughs. "So I guess you haven't visited me much because you're grounded."

I almost tell him then, just to get it over with. "And because of Luke."

"Do you miss him?"

I nod, and Dave asks why I won't take him back. I shake my head. "You almost finished your car?"

"Take you for a ride in it, Rosie, when I'm done. Charlie's grandpa offered me work on the weekends when my summer job at the garage is over. Should have enough money to put a new engine in."

"You haven't kissed her yet?"

"She doesn't talk about me?"

"Can you believe she has other things to say?"

"She talks about the strangest stuff. You know, she told me about this guy who set fire to his guitar. Sacrificed it even though he'd painted it and thought it was a beauty."

"Why?"

"I don't know. She told me, but I was too busy thinking about kissing her. So, are you coming to the talent quest? I'll break you out if I have to."

"You'd do that, wouldn't you?"

"I'd do anything for you," he says. I know he would. Luke would have, too, only I pushed him away. Charlie as well.

"I have to go." I kiss him on the cheek.

I take the long way home. The way with punishing hills. I ride fast so it hurts. Mum's peeling potatoes when I walk in. "Can I go to the talent quest?" I ask.

"You should go. You should face up to Charlie. Face up to Dave."

"You're right," I say, and she puts the potato she's holding into the sink.

I call Dave at the hospital. "Mum says I can go. I'll meet you there."

"We have to keep up the tradition of giving shit to everyone in that thing," he says.

"Antony and his brothers do enough of that for the whole town. I saw him buying stuff to throw. Says he's smuggling it into the place in his underwear. The guy's crazy."

"Yeah," Dave says. "But so's anyone who gets on that stage."

Charlie

I finish my song today. It's strange, sure. But not entirely un-beautiful. I sing it without my guitar for Grandpa while we're clearing Gran's path before the concert. Actually, I sing it while I clear the path, and he walks behind, telling me what's a weed and what's not. "It's lovely," he says. "She's proud."

"You still talk to Gran?"

"Every day. Last night we talked about the first holiday we ever had. It was before we were married, so she stayed in a room at one end of the hotel and I stayed in one at the other. I told her that story, the day I watched her die. I didn't think she'd heard me until last night."

I'd never thought before that Grandpa was with Gran when she died, that he'd held her hand as she fell away from him. It must have been hard for him to know that he couldn't catch her. I never thought before how hard it must have been for Dad because he didn't get to hold Mum's hand. Maybe that's why he's been so sad so long.

Grandpa stares out past the red flowers to the mountains. I look, too, and think about Dad and Mum and Gran and Grandpa and how it hurts to lose someone you should be able to keep. You can't live worrying that you're going to lose people, though. You can't live worrying.

"Are you nervous about tonight?" Grandpa asks.

"I've got a feeling I might not stuff up," I say. And we keep weeding the path till we can see clearly that view of the mountains, purple and blue in the distance.

"You'll be great," Dahlia says before I've even said hi.

"How did you know it was me?"

"I didn't. So far tonight I've told my sister's boyfriend and two telemarketers that they'll be great. What are you wearing?"

"That blue dress we bought at the place that time."

"Very hot. Your hair's up?"

"Yep."

"You're still singing that song you sang the other day?"

"Yep."

"You sound nervous. Don't be nervous."

"I felt like a rock star this morning for about three minutes."

"Think about those three minutes while you're onstage."

"I was in the shower. Naked."

"It works better the other way. You imagine you're clothed and they're naked. Wait, Dave's in the audience, right? Your grandpa, too? Maybe your dad?"

"Yep."

"Okay. No one's naked. Keep it reality-based. You're Charlie Duskin with a killer voice. And call me after."

"I thought you were going out with Louise?"

"I am, but I'm keeping my mobile phone on, so call me. Whatever happens."

"Even if it's a new experience in humiliation?"

"Especially if it's a new experience in humiliation," she says. "Oh, and, Charlie, remember what you say to anyone who doesn't like your music?"

"Shove it up your butt."

I put down the phone while she's still cracking herself up in the background singing about butts. They'll let anyone into the in-crowd these days.

I leave a note for Dad telling him to meet us at the concert. I grab my guitar and my grandpa. "You ready?" he asks.

"Yep."

"Rock on," he says. "That was a little message from your gran."

"You think Dad'll come?"

"He'll come. Your gran and I didn't raise an idiot." He looks at me. "Neither did your mother and father."

"I know," I say, and do a last check of me in the mirror. Not entirely unsexy. Okay. "Let's roll."

Rose

Luke and Dave are in the second row when I arrive. Antony
Barellan and his mates are in the front, sneaking eggs out of
their underwear. The Barellan kids aren't the only ones getting ready to yell and throw, either. It's a tradition in this
town. By the time the acts start, the place will be packed.

"Rose!" Dave calls, and points at a seat next to him. Luke
doesn't say anything. He doesn't even turn around. I shuffle
past the other kids. "Charlie not here yet?" I ask. A glass
smashing makes me jump.

"Not yet." Dave passes me a packet of chips. "Everyone
else in town is, though." He looks behind him. "I reckon
there's at least a hundred."

"A hundred and fifty," Luke says, and the two of them start

punching each other as if the one who hits the hardest will be right.

"Oh God," I say.

"What? Your mother doing her Madonna act again?" Antony turns around from his spot in front of me. I ignore him and point to the board next to the stage. Dave's and Luke's eyes find what mine have. "Shit," Dave says.

"Uh-uh." Luke shakes his head, turning round to check out the packed pub again. "I think you mean 'Fuck.'"

Charlie's name is written in red chalk on the board. She's act number two, in front of Mrs. Danon and her dancing dog, Elvin. "What do you know?" Antony says. "Two dogs in a row."

"We have to stop her," I say.

"Maybe the crowd will like her act." Dave's too hopeful for his own good. "It doesn't say what she's planning on singing."

"The blues." I point at the long row of Barellan kids and their friends. A local talent quest is something no self-respecting kid does, at least not in our town. Charlie's come a long way in the self-respect department lately. It's my fault she's getting up there. I've driven her over the edge.

"Maybe she really can sing and play the guitar," Dave says.

"You ever heard her?" I ask.

"No. But just because we never heard her doesn't mean she can't."

"Yes it does, Dave. People who are good at things do them. Charlie's been pretending she can play the guitar and write songs and sing because she wants people to like her."

"That doesn't make sense. Why would she get up there in front of everyone if she can't play?"

And finally I've reached the moment of truth. "She'd humiliate herself to prove something to me."

"I don't get it. Why would she do that?"

"The same reason she stole the cigarettes and went with Luke and Antony to the quarry. She thinks I used her."

"But why would she think that now?"

"I can explain later, but we have to stop her from getting up there."

"Tell me now, Rose."

I don't even know where to start. "Mrs. Wesson helped me apply for this scholarship last year, and I got it. But I needed someone to help me get to the city. Mum and Dad were always at me to hang out with Charlie. I needed to go so badly. . . ."

"And you thought Charlie would be the perfect ride out of here." He finishes my sentence for me. "I asked you so many times."

"I only lied at the start."

"As if that matters. You've got everything. A great family. Friends. Charlie had nothing. She trusted you."

"I'm sorry."

"Sorry you got caught."

Dave's yelling and Antony's laughing and Luke's watching and I want to run. I want to leave this place where the local talent quest and someone who wants something bigger than here, bigger than themselves, are the jokes of the town. But if I run, then Charlie gets on that stage. Better me on fire than her. Dave looks at Antony shining an egg on his trousers like it's a cricket ball. "If that hits her, it's your fault."

Luke leans across Dave and takes hold of my hand. "Easy. She made a few mistakes."

"Well, it's time she fixed them." Dave pushes me up. "We're going backstage."

"Are you coming, Luke?" I ask.

"I've got something I need to do here. You'll be okay, Rosie," he says. I walk with my eyes on my feet so I don't trip.

When we get backstage, the first act has started and the crowd's laughing. Charlie's sitting between Mrs. Danon and Elvin, looking like she's realized the clear blue ocean she's about to go swimming in is swarming with sharks.

Dave catches me by the arm and drags me around the corner before I can speak. "Tell her she can do it," he says.

"What?"

"Go back and tell her she can do it."

"You've seen what happens to people on that stage, Dave. Antony's in the middle of the front row. If Charlie goes out there, she's dead."

"She's dead if she doesn't," he says. "Tell her she can do it, Rose."

I move back to where I can see Charlie. She's reaching for her guitar with nervous hands. I walk toward her as the first act slides past us off the stage. "Hey. You're probably still mad, but I wanted to say good luck."

"I'm more nervous than mad now." She stares through the curtain. "I think Antony has an egg."

"He does. It's his brain."

"He took it out of his pants."

"Like I said, it's his brain."

She laughs. "Shit. My hands are shaking. You think I should go out there?"

Dave hovers in the background. I turn my back so it's me and her. "Do you think you can do this? You're not lying like you did about Dahlia?" It's brutal, but brutal's what it is. Better to face this now than out there. "I don't care. If you let me, I'll be your friend either way."

She looks at me and at Dave. She looks out the curtain and strums her guitar. "Yeah," she says. "Oh yeah. This I can do."

"Then I think you should go out there."

Dave walks over as they announce, "The lovely Charlie Duskin."

"Don't look so nervous, you two," she says, and goes onstage.

We watch her walk into the spotlight she's been hiding from most of her life. Sure, friendship is all about believing in someone so hard they believe it, too. Sure, it's about trust. But if anyone hurts her tonight, it's about ripping them apart with my bare hands and really enjoying it.

"You tell her she could do it?" Dave asks.

"She told me. She's got a little attitude going on."

"Hi, everyone. My name's Charlie Duskin. And this," she says, smiling, "is a song I wrote for tonight."

For a second, I think it's going to be okay. Charlie doesn't look new out there. She looks like she's lived forever and this is the test of how much she knows. But then she strikes up the first chord, and her hand slips on the strings.

"Get on with it!" Antony yells. "I'm bored already."

Her hand slips again.

"Charlie Dorkin thinks she can sing," he calls. If I could reverse time and take back that stupid name, I'd do it. I'd give up my scholarship. I'd stay in this town forever if only Charlie would sing right now and shut Antony Barellan up for the rest of his dumb life.

She sucks in her breath. That guitar hangs round her neck like a noose. Dave stands next to me with his hands in fists. "You better hope she starts," he says. "Because if she doesn't, I'm going out there and you're backup."

Dave knows two songs all the way through. "J.Lo?" I ask.

"Beyoncé."

"Shit."

"We will be," he says, and then the smallest sound starts.

It's so soft at first that it's hidden under yelling and glasses clinking. It's like feeling the cool change come through your window on a night when you're hungry for a summer breeze. It's singing the color of sunrise. I've never heard anything like it before, sad and hopeful at the same time, like the beginning and the end all mixed in together.

"She's amazing," I say, half not believing it. They're still calling out stuff over the top of her. She slowly gets louder. Her voice is sweet and even. She knows what she wants to say, and she's saying it.

Before she's finished, the whole place is quiet. "I thought

that stuff only happened in the movies." Dave doesn't answer. It's hard to talk with your mouth hanging open. He's got it bad for her, and I can see why. Charlie makes all of us look like shadows tonight. It's not just because her song is funny and sad and beautiful. It's because *she's* all of those things, too. That's kind of hard to resist.

When she's finished, she takes her guitar off and looks out into the audience. I think everyone's still in shock that such a big voice came from the shiest person in the room. "Shove that up your arse, Antony Barellan," she says into the microphone, and the whole place goes wild. Charlie's a little late for Antony, though. She was too caught up in her song to notice that he went quiet before the end. Luke grabbed him by the collar and dragged him out the back. It's why I started applauding way too early.

Charlie

I walk onstage thinking, Okay, if I fall, there's going to be crushing pain and more than a little humiliation. But so what? Life's a bit of a high-wire act. And then I get out there and look at the crowd looking at me and I think, So this is what it feels like to be alive. This is what it's like to have sound that echoes round the walls and makes people listen. "Let loose once in a while, kid," Gus always says. "You'll be the biz."

And I am. Sure, my fingers slip a little across the strings. Not ideal, but understandable. There's a guy in the front row about to throw an egg at me. I could get louder and cover Antony; I could drown him with heavy chords. But that's not the song I planned to play tonight.

I let my guitar tease at the air for a bit, let it circle, let my voice kick in. I throw it out to the crowd, throw chords into their throats and they catch them. I throw it all straight out of that part of me that hopes for things. That wants for things. At the end my voice rises and I see in their faces that I'm playing the crowd. I'm reaching in and playing them. "What are we waiting for? Love to pay a visit? Say it's not so fucking hard, is it? To work out what I'm doing at the door?"

And while I'm playing and singing, I've got a few things floating around my head. I've got Grandpa's voice saying something about punishment and books that won't ever balance. I've got his voice telling Dad that he couldn't have known. I think I know what Grandpa meant by that. I can almost touch the thought. It's something to do with what happens when people die. A thought about patchy paddocks, dry, with nothing living underneath. Until something rises up and starts in them, and they get on with the business of living. Grandpa loved Gran, but he's getting on with it. If you stay burned out and over for seven years, then there's a reason. I think I know what it is now.

I look up after the last chord and smile. I tell Antony Barellan to shove it up his arse, and I see Dad clapping his hands off. I give him a little wave to show him that it's okay to be happy. I give him a little smile to show him what it looks like.

"You did it, you fucking did it!" Dave and Rose yell as I walk offstage. I want to stay with them. I want to talk all night to Dave and then kiss him. I want to sing a few songs just for him. There's something I have to do first, though.

"You get that from your mother," Dad says when I walk over.

"But I get the ability to make great toast from you," I tell him. Grandpa gives me some love and then leaves us. The crowd goes a little wild again and then stops. Dad and I go.

We walk on instinct, without words. She's all around us, voice moving in the leaves and rocks and water and dirt and air. We're breathing her in. We sit at the river, and she shines on our skin, and we just soak her up. "Do you remember that fund-raising concert?" I ask.

"It's hard to forget losing the power of speech in front of two hundred primary-school children."

"The way Mum opened your mouth and sang."

He chuckles, and she's there with us, rolling with laughter like she did that day. Dad rocks back and forth, tears falling out of him he's laughing so hard. When we've finished, I move a little closer, and he doesn't move away, so I move a little closer still.

"When Arrie and I were kids, we came here all the time," he says. "We went to the falls, too. But it was right at this spot I asked her to marry me." Dad drifts his feet through the water for a long time. He takes off his glasses and drifts them, too. Cleans them on his shirt.

"It was my fault she died," he says finally, and his words are in a key I've never heard. Sadder than E minor, even. They're in the key of A minor, A for Arabella.

"I started a new job that day. I couldn't eat; my stomach was turning. 'Just have some toast,' she said, and I snapped at her. It was the nerves talking. It was my first big city job. I blamed her when I couldn't find two of my knives. 'Stop moving my things,' I said. I found them on the way out, sitting on the kitchen bench. I didn't tell her."

A few leaves fall and the wind floats them round. "She was bringing you knives."

"I didn't even need them." He lowers his head. "My sweet Arabella. You should have stayed home."

We sit side by side in the night. "It was an accident," I say. "She knows it."

"You and her," he says. "The two best things to ever happen to me. She would have loved seeing you up there tonight."

"I was not entirely uncool."

"You definitely weren't. Dave Robbie thought so."

"He is not entirely uncool, either."

"I'm very glad that boy lives a long drive from your bedroom."

"There'll be other boys," I say. "Loads of boys, lining up." I pat him on the back. "Just making up for some lost time."

"Don't feel like you have to do that," he says.

We sit awhile longer, listening and breathing her in because we know that on the walk out it's going to get quiet. The leaves and the water won't make so much noise. The quiet of living without her might take some time to get used to. We're ready for it, though. Ready Duskins.

"I love you, Charlotte," Dad says after a while, taking his feet out of the water and brushing the dirt from his hands.

He moves closer this time, and it's enough so that we touch. "I love you, too," I say. No wonder the whole world writes songs about those words.

Dave's circling his bike around the front of the shop when we get home. Rose's bike is leaning against the fence. Dad stares at him and says, "Be back by twelve, Charlotte. I'll be waiting up."

"I don't think he's ever really looked at me before," Dave says. "He's kind of scary."

"He says he was a country boy like you once. He knows what you're thinking."

"Nah, he doesn't." Dave looks at the ground and grins. "I'd be dead."

"You want to go for a ride?" I ask. "Maybe back to where we were the other night?"

"I was thinking somewhere not that far," he says.

We ride along the road together. There are no hills. Flat stretches out on either side of us. Wheels whir in the night; light pushes at the dark as we move forward. He takes a side road and stops at the footy field. "Short grass, no snakes," he says. We walk over and climb the scoreboard.

Dave reaches into his bag and hands me a little trophy.

"I won?"

"You did. Rose accepted on your behalf to cracking applause. I've never seen anything like you up there."

"It's not very big, is it?" I hold up the trophy.

"Shiny, though," Dave says. "I think it's left over from the award night at the footy."

"You ever get one?"

"I never scored," he says. "Not once in the whole season."

"Don't worry," I say. "I have a feeling you'll score tonight."

He laughs. "Who are you?"

"Charlie Duskin," I say. "Trophy winner. A not-uncool girl."

And then we're at that moment where you both go and get what you want or you both go back. The moment when you say, Stuff being scared; what's on the other side is better. That moment when you inch closer to each other little by little, till your skin starts and ends in the same place. Till your faces get so close your lips start and end in the same place, too. Till you taste milk shake and salt and sugar days and the world spins and the stars sound like harmonicas.

"Boys are easy," I say after my first kiss. "They're kind of like guitars, without the strings."

"If I compared you to a car right now, Rose'd say I was insensitive."

"I think it's time we said whatever it is we want."

He leans in and the bird on his wrist flaps against my neck and his mouth is warm and the inside of me goes harmonic this time and the whole thing is a million times better than what I imagined. And I imagined it pretty good.

"Sing something," he says.

I sing him a little version of the song I've been working on. "Love's a funny song. The words don't make much sense, and the beat comes out all wrong. But it goes a little like this. Sweet, fever, mandolin. Our laughter caving in. Tongues and wanting. Bliss."

"Nice," he says.

Slowly

So slowly, really slowly
I'm all the chords there are

So slowly, really slowly
I'm keys I never heard

So slowly, really slowly
I'm spinning song and dancing
Rising voice beneath my skin

Rose

Charlie's left by the time they announce she's won. I go on-stage and hold up that crappy little football trophy like it's a national music award while everyone claps.

And then five minutes after the whole thing's done, everyone's gone. Mum and Dad drove home. Dave went to wait for Charlie. Antony doesn't have the concentration span to hold a grudge, so Luke probably left with him and his brothers.

I sit outside for a while, staring over the grass, thinking about Dave's face when he was watching Charlie. Wondering if he'll forgive me.

Luke walks around the side and sits next to me. "I thought you left," I say.

"You thought wrong." He swings his legs. "She was good. I never knew she could sing."

"Me neither."

He leans back and looks at the sky. "So your parents found out, huh? Dave says you're grounded for life."

"I'm grounded in the afterlife."

"I can't believe you cut class and went to the city. It would have been more fun with Dave and me along."

"I've never been there, but I don't think prison's fun."

"You always do that," he says. "Make out like I'm headed for jail. Like I'm not smart enough to end up anywhere else."

"You do so many stupid things," I say.

"You do them, too; I just never make a big deal about it."

It's hard to argue with him about that after this summer. "I don't think you're stupid," I say. "I don't. I think you're careless. I think—"

He covers my mouth. "For once, Rosie, just say, 'You are right, Luke.' Say it."

He moves his hand a little. "I think maybe."

He puts it back. "They're not the three magic words."

He takes his hand away again and I say, "Let's have sex."

"You just can't say I'm right. You know one day I'll find a girl who is willing to do it with me, and I'll forget all about you."

"You're right," I tell him, but I don't feel so good admitting it.

He holds my hand and pulls me back so we can both see the sky. "Nah, Rosie," he says. "I'm not right about that."

* * *

"Dave?" I knock on his window. It's barely light, but I couldn't sleep. He sticks his head through. "What do you want?" he asks. I hold up a car magazine. "Come inside," he says, and I crawl through the window.

I lie next to him. "I should have told you about the scholarship."

"You should have told Charlie."

"It's hard to explain why I kept it from you. I think maybe telling you would have made it real. I think—"

"You thought telling me would have stuffed up your plan with Charlie. And you thought I would have told Luke, and he would have stuffed it up even more."

"I guess it's not so hard to explain."

"You're not the only one with plans, Rose."

"You want to be a mechanic," I say. "I listen."

"I want to *design* cars, and don't look so surprised. You're not the only one who wants to get out of here."

I sit up close to the window so I can feel the breeze. "Do you forgive me?"

"You and Luke are my best mates. We've been fighting all our lives."

"I know."

"You're just pissed because you're in the wrong this time."

"I know that, too." I lean back. We drift into sleep and dream separate things.

"Hey," Luke says from the window, waking us up. "I'm gone for a bit and you start getting on with my girlfriend. In bed."

"I heard she's not your girlfriend anymore," Dave says.

"I was talking to Rose," he answers, crawling in the window and diving between us. He and Dave wrestle. "Davey's got a girlfriend of his own now," Luke says, and we laugh, and I tell them they're idiots till Mr. Robbie yells for us to shut up. "Just ignore him," Dave says, and smacks Luke in the face with a pillow.

Charlie

"I thought I'd find you here," I say, and sit next to Rose at the edge of the freeway. "So this is what the view looks like from this place."

"Best spot to dream about leaving," she says, ripping at the corner of her nail. "Which is all I'll be doing this year. Mum and Dad are too pissed now to even talk about the scholarship. Mum barely talks at all."

"You'll be eighteen in a couple of years. Is it so bad to stay here till then?"

"You know the feeling you get when you're homesick? Things are going great, and then all of a sudden your stomach's saying, This isn't the place you're meant to be. That's how I feel all the time."

"Did you tell your mum and dad that?"

"They won't listen."

I'd take her with me if I could. I asked Dad, and he said it was up to Mrs. Butler. It's awful being trapped somewhere you don't want to be. "Rose, close your eyes and listen."

"Why?"

"Listen to the cars." We're quiet as the trucks crash past us and fade, one after the other. "Hear that sound?"

"I've been listening to cars and trucks forever."

"Listen beneath it, sort of. Hear it rising and falling? That's the sound of the ocean. That's the sound of waves."

"It's the sound of people leaving, Charlie."

"Listen more closely, really listen."

She closes her eyes again and leans her whole body toward the road. Sometimes sounds can have more than one meaning. Before this summer, the sound of trucks reminded me of Mum dying.

"I know what you mean," she says. "But it's not enough."

I guess life's never perfect, not for me and Dad, not even for the Rose Butlers of the world.

"So when do you leave?" she asks.

"Tomorrow. Dad and I decided we need a new start. He's going back early to look for a job with fewer hours, one where he only works during the day."

"I'm happy, but I'll miss you, Charlie. The start of the summer seems years ago."

"We'll visit each other. You can come and stay with me in the holidays. I asked Dad. He said he'd talk to your mum."

"Really? Dave might want to come, too."

"Did he tell you we kissed?"

"Some things a guy doesn't have to say."

"It was a thousand times better than how I imagined it, and I've got a great imagination. Is that how it was with you and Luke?"

"Yep," she says, and we think about that for a while.

"So it's not all bad in this town, then," I say.

"Not all bad. That's what scares me."

"I don't think we have to end up like anyone except us," I say, and she nods.

I leave before she does. "Look for me at the side of the road tomorrow morning, Charlie. I'll be waving."

"Look for me in the car. I'll be waving back."

"Hi, Mrs. Butler. Can I come in?"

I don't even get to say the whole speech I planned about Rose and why she wants to go to the city and how I'll look after her. I say the first bit, about how I miss Mum and I wish that she was here so that I could tell her stuff, and Mrs. Butler's hands start checking in her sleeves for tissues.

"She'll be at the side of the freeway at about seven o'clock," I tell her. "I can show you the spot on a map—"

"I don't need a map," she says. "I know how to get there."

Dad's closing the shop for the day when I leave the Butlers' house. "You're finishing early."

"It's our last night in town," he says. "I thought I'd make some Grandpa Gnocchi for dinner and Charlotte Chocolate Mousse for dessert."

Dad looks sad still. But he's trying, and he gets loads of

points for that. I've put my iPod away for a little while so I don't miss him talking when he gets the urge. "They're good names," I tell him. "What about some Dave Robbie Antipasto?"

He frowns. "I invited Dave. But I'm not naming a dish after him."

"Fair enough." Dad's as friendly as he can be with the guy who's kissing his daughter, and it feels good to be over-protected again.

After dinner, Dad and Grandpa leave Dave and me alone. I give him his CD. "I'll listen to it tomorrow at the score-board," he says.

We do some half dancing, and we talk a little about Fozzie toothbrushes and designing cars, and we come up with fifty things to do when you're missing someone that don't involve kissing someone else.

"'Kissing' is a funny word," he says.

"It is. But I like it," I tell him, and he looks at me like I've been waiting to be looked at, and it's nothing like how Luke looks at Rose. It's a cello look. A song played late at night by wishful fingers. Wishful fingers covered in car oil. More important: it's a look that's all about me.

"There's a song about you on that CD," I say.

"How will I know which one?"

"Trust me. You'll know." Maybe it's desperate, Louise. But I just don't care. And neither does he.

This Is a Song About Dave

I like the little shadows
You got sitting in your smile
I could watch them for a while
Quite a long while, actually

I like how I never had the call before
To use the word "adore" before
But now I do

I got a little piece of what I want with you

I like how you don't score
At football, or with girls
Except for me
I think we should keep it that way

I like how you say
I'm fucking gorgeous and shake
Off years of ordinary
Cover me with extraordinary
Ways of seeing I never saw before
But now I do

I got a little piece of what I want with you

Rose

The air is warm this morning. It's going to be a beautiful day. It's funny how the weather takes no notice of how you feel. Things just are how they are, I guess, and you can't change them.

I keep a lookout for the old blue Ford, even though I know they won't be leaving for a while yet. Luke and Dave and I are planning to hang out this afternoon, and I'm glad. The day would be empty without them.

There's rustling behind me, but instead of Luke, it's Mum. "What are you doing here?" I ask.

"I came to find you," she says.

"Well, here I am."

"And where's that?" She eases herself down next to me.

"I don't know." I keep watching the cars.

"Most people's lives look better than your own," she says. "Most other parents look better than your own."

"I only said those things because I was mad. I don't want you dead."

"That's a relief." She shifts closer and watches with me. "I wanted to give you such a good life."

I have to tell her how it is, or I'll be sitting here forever. "You have. But you and Dad used to be different. We read books and went for walks. But then you started working all the time. The old you would have let me go to the city. Don't you remember what it was like to be excited?"

"Of course I remember. I felt it when I found out I was pregnant with you. I fought with my parents and told them nothing was going to stop me raising you. We were one person then."

"But we're not now. I want to be at that school. I want to learn things, read books, and have people talk to me about them." I let out that thing I've been keeping in. "I don't want to get pregnant by Luke and never leave here."

She sucks in her breath. "Is there a real chance of that?"

"Not yet."

She lets her breath out. "God. That's a relief. I guess we haven't talked much about anything lately." She plays with a button on her cardigan and her face sags.

"Mum, don't cry."

"I wanted to talk, when I knew things weren't right for you. But you're so much like me, Rosie. When things go wrong, the barriers go up, and it takes an army to get through. I was just too tired to try."

"Me going doesn't mean I don't love you. It doesn't mean I won't come back." The whole time we've been talking, the sky has been feeding on the sun.

"Okay, Rosie Butler," Mum says. "We'll work out a way." She loops her fingers through mine. "You'd better come back once in a while."

"I can go?"

She nods, and the sky explodes around the two of us. The world is fat with color. "I'll come back and tell you all about school and the city and the things I'm doing there." I stop. "Who's going to tell Dad?"

"He knows. We made plans last night. 'You have to let her go,' he said, 'or she'll rip you in two.'" She laughs and wipes a few tears. "It's hard to let you go."

It feels good to hold Mum's hand today. "I can't wait to see the world," I tell her.

"I couldn't either at your age."

"What happened?" I ask.

"I get to choose my life, too, you know."

I think about that. "You choose working in a caravan park?"

She grabs me and pulls me close and smacks a kiss on my face. "I choose you and your dad and my friends and this gorgeous place." She smacks another kiss. "There's Charlie," she says, and points at the old car making its way home. I raise my hand and wave. I know that she's doing the same thing.

After the car has disappeared, I keep staring. "What are you looking at?" Mum asks.

I point ahead. "Those mountains at the back of the freeway."

"The light makes them change color during the day," she says. "You never noticed that?"

"I guess I never looked that closely. They're pretty amazing."

"You're smiling again," Mum says. "That's nice."

"I can't help it," I answer. "There's so much to look forward to."

Charlie

I see two small figures at the edge of the freeway, and I know it's Rose and her mum. I wave till they're dots in the distance. Goodbyes are hard, but I'm not saying goodbye. I'll be back. "See you next time, Charlie Brown," Grandpa said when I kissed him.

The sun's behind Dad and me when we leave this morning. I keep my eyes open. I smile at Dad. I smile at the thought of Dave sitting on the scoreboard listening to me. We pass that skeleton tree, bare branches covered in birds now, and I smile at the road ahead.

Acknowledgments

Thank you very much, Knopf Books for Young Readers. Special thanks to my editor, Allison Wortche—*A Little Wanting Song* has greatly benefited from your care and insight. Thank you, Pan Macmillan, especially Anna McFarlane, Brianne Tunnicliffe, Jo Jarrah, and Cate Paterson. And lastly, thank you to all the friends and family who let me talk constantly about Rose, Luke, Dave, and Charlie as if they were real.

Cath Crowley grew up in rural Victoria, Australia. She studied professional writing and editing at the Royal Melbourne Institute of Technology and works as both a freelance writer and a part-time teacher in Melbourne. *A Little Wanting Song* was short-listed for the Children's Book Council of Australia Book of the Year Award.

To find out more about Cath, visit www.cathcrowley.com.au.